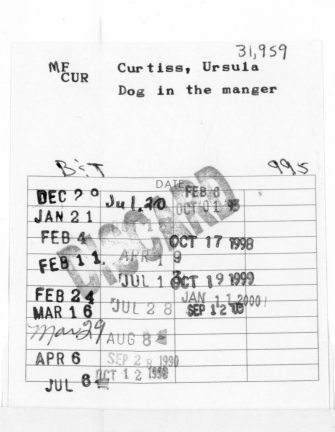

31,959

MF
CUR  Curtiss, Ursula
      Dog in the manger

B&T                    99.5

DATE

| DEC 2 0 | Jul 20 | FEB 8 | |
| JAN 2 1 | | OCT 01 98 | |
| FEB 4 | | OCT 17 1998 | |
| FEB 1 1 | APR 1 9 | | |
| FEB 24 | JUL 1 | OCT 19 1999 | |
| MAR 1 6 | JUL 2 8 | JAN 1 1 2000 | |
| Mar 29 | AUG 8 | SEP 1 2 05 | |
| APR 6 | SEP 2 8 1990 | | |
| JUL 6 | OCT 1 2 1998 | | |

DISCARD

# Dog
# in
# the
# Manger

# Dog in the Manger

A NOVEL OF SUSPENSE

## Ursula Curtiss

DODD, MEAD & COMPANY
NEW YORK

1  2  3  4  5  6  7  8  9  10

Library of Congress Cataloging in Publication Data

Curtiss, Ursula Reilly.
  Dog in the manger.

  I. Title.
PS3505.U915D6        813'.54        82–1501
ISBN 0–396–08057–X                  AACR2

*To my daughter*
*Ursula Mary Curtiss*

# Dog
# in
# the
# Manger

# Chapter
# One

It was on an evening in October that Mrs. Ivy first wore, for eyes other than her own, the new earrings that were to cast such a long and killing shadow.

They were not diamond pendants or emeralds set in gold or any other tempting arrangement of precious stones in precious metal. They were tailored, white, enamellike buttons, perhaps a trifle oversized but otherwise unremarkable. Inside their backs, a fact known only to her and the audiologist, were tiny hearing aids.

In spite of practice in front of the television set and on the telephone, Mrs. Ivy felt queerly self-conscious, a sensation alien to her, about the imminent arrival of her two nephews and her niece, all the close family she had. After two years of increasing deafness, reentry into the world of real sound was jarring and almost painful. Her own footsteps, previously communicated to her chiefly by vibration, were so startling that she found herself watching her feet with some anxiety.

Cars pulled into the driveway, punctual as always—they

knew she did not care to be kept waiting—and Roger uncurled his peculiar length from his basket and emitted a dutiful rush of barks. It was the only volume in the house uncontrollable by the turn of a button, but Mrs. Ivy assumed that she would get used to it.

Nan was first over the threshold, calling a loud, gay, "Hi! *What* a night," as her brothers came in behind her and closed the door on the leaf-rattling wind. She kissed her aunt's cheek and bent to pat the dog, who did not see a great many people and was therefore inclined to make the most of them. "Hello, Roger, hello, good boy."

Why this embarrassment, wondered Mrs. Ivy as she was kissed in turn by Laurence and Donald; almost as if she were about to announce her intention of marrying a man half her age? It wasn't as though they hadn't been dropping tactful references for months about new technology in hearing aids.

Or was that it, plain and simple? "We finally persuaded old Aunt Charlotte . . . " Whereas Charlotte Ivy was in the habit of being a law unto herself.

Get it over with. Mrs. Ivy had proceeded as far as "I want you all to observe" and was actually lifting a hand when, quite close to her and in a voice dropped to one of private loathing, Nan said to Roger, "Don't *lick*, you ghastly beast."

And, in a continuation of the lightning flashing down Mrs. Ivy's personal sky, Laurence turned to hang up his coat. Safely profiled against lip-reading, he said rapidly in the same quiet tone that would have been completely inaudible two weeks ago, "Watch it, I think she just gave you a sharp look."

At that, Donald put down Mrs. Ivy's current library book, the jacket of which he had been inspecting idly, and the three of them gazed at her, waiting courteously for whatever it was she wanted them to observe.

"My fire," said Mrs. Ivy, nodding at the end of the room. "The first of the season."

It wasn't entrapment at that moment, it was an evasion made

out of genuine surprise and a trace of anger. True, with his bright terrier face and his short-legged, fringy fawn body, which went on and on until it arrived at his tail, Roger was not the dog of anyone's dreams—but he was there at all because they had insisted that it wasn't safe for Mrs. Ivy, living alone, to go unwarned of any surreptitious approach from without, and Nan in particular had made much of him.

At first, with an eye to her rugs and her antique bottle-green loveseat, Mrs. Ivy had said that she would rather have burglars than a dog. The seed flourished, however—what if on one of the days Hattie Callahan did not come, she should be reading or writing letters in the living room while someone was letting himself in at the back door?—and she had finally entrusted to Donald, who had more time on his hands than Laurence, the mission of acquiring a dog of a barking nature.

From the animal shelter, she specified, because that way everybody would benefit. Out of common humanity, she also asked for the least adoptable; it wasn't a pet she wanted, but an alarm system. Donald had taken her at her word and produced Roger, the strange mixture of terrier, perhaps Yorkshire, and long-haired dachshund.

For all her resolution, Mrs. Ivy had grown stealthily fond of him, and bought him a basket and toys. He was not a nuisance with them; he played gravely by himself with his hard rubber ring and squeaky objects and rawhide bones, as if well aware that these diversions were the equivalent of coffee breaks for humans. Nor were the toys a hazard for her feet; he always returned them neatly to his basket.

There was no law that said that Nan or anyone else had to like him, but the depth of her aversion under her pretense of affection was somehow shocking—and to that had to be added Laurence's swift and quiet complicity. What other views had been expressed while she sat in her deafness, providing them with drinks and nuts and cheese and crackers every few weeks?

"Here you are, Aunt Charlotte." Martini placed beside her,

glasses delivered to Nan and Donald. Laurence, the oldest and consequently playing host with a hint of importance, raised his own, said loudly, "Cheers," and sat down.

And, in the second step of the ritual, Mrs. Ivy said, "Well. Tell me what you've all been up to."

An ironic phrase, tonight, but the expected one and with the expected response. Nan, sitting under a lamp that illuminated her lips and speaking with strong-pitched enunciation, said, "Peter got the promotion he was hoping for, isn't that nice? Of course, it will mean . . ."

Mrs. Ivy listened and nodded, remembering to watch closely and turn her head occasionally as if for better reception. She reflected that they were a good-looking lot, with their longish, straight noses—she almost touched her own, which was exactly the same—and grayed-blue eyes in startling contrast to warm skin that spoke of the west coast of Ireland.

Well, her late and much younger brother, Clement, had been a very attractive man. Odd how genes skipped around: Hattie Callahan, who was Mrs. Ivy's second cousin, had next to nothing in the way of nose and a sturdy but undistinguished shape. Whenever invited to join these gatherings, more as a gesture than anything else, she said bluntly, "No, thanks, they make me nervous."

Mrs. Ivy realized that Laurence had stopped roaring at her and Donald, whose turn it was, was spreading his hands, shaking his dark head, and smiling. The odd man out in that trio, the one who had produced a novel two years ago and taken strange temporary jobs ever since. Mrs. Ivy smiled back at him and let a peaceful silence fall.

Neither Laurence's wife nor Nan's husband came for drinks more than a few times a year, which was eminently understandable; purely social conversation could not survive having to be repeated once and sometimes twice. Family, at least in theory, could sit and contemplate without stress.

But the ability to hear must have something to do with acuity of vision, because to Mrs. Ivy Nan's gaze was resting with something just short of acquisitiveness on the small, graceful desk in the corner, and Laurence was studying the lamplit glow of the Royal Sarouk as if visualizing it on another and more familiar floor.

He was a stockbroker, and it occurred to Mrs. Ivy that it would really fetch him if she proposed buying gold in the current market. It did, to such an extent that it was Donald who went out to make fresh drinks.

At the end of Laurence's imploring advice to stay with her blue-chip stocks, Mrs. Ivy excused herself to turn on the oven for her dinner. Her newly restored aural perception cut through all kinds of fogs, and her much brisker step had carried her halfway back through the dining room when she stopped.

Laurence was saying casually, "Does anybody else get the impression that she's a trifle cool? That business about buying gold was practically a threat."

"If you mean because of me and Roger, don't be silly, you know she can't hear," said Nan, defensive. "It's just one of those crotchets old people get." Her fleeting pause seemed to contain a wry movement of the mouth corners. "As somebody observed, 'Men may come and men may go, but I go on forever.' "

"Nan," said Donald on a note of protest, but he was mild about it.

"I still think there's something in the air," said Laurence, "and if we have any brains we'll straighten up. But first, where do you suppose she finds this terrible Scotch?"

"A penny saved is a penny to put into blue chips," said Nan.

Somehow, Mrs. Ivy contained her wrath until they were gone.

She was not really cut to the heart. At seventy-seven she was sensible if not actually cynical, and knew at bottom that because of the great age gap there had always been a mutual aspect to these arrangements. They were interested in her estate, naturally enough, and for her part it was pleasant to have some attractive, guaranteed attention.

But to be looked upon as a dinosaur, without the grace to become extinct?

What other comments had passed among them, over two years and conceivably while she was in the room with them? Slightly dangerous fun, with a head a little turned and an answering smile directed at the rug or a window. Mrs. Ivy was thoroughly sure that tonight's revelation was an iceberg's tip.

She was angry in a clear and balanced way that took into account the suggestion (dropped at once when she refused) that she close off the upstairs of the house in which she had lived the fifty years of her married life and turn her late husband's study into a bedroom. "Much safer, Aunt Charlotte, and you'd save a fortune in heating bills."

Their fortune.

It had been difficult to resist confronting at least two of them: "I don't know about forever, Nan, but granted reasonable health it's either a fool or a coward who doesn't go on as long as he can." And to Laurence, "I see no real reason why I should provide you with pinchbottle."

A triumph, but too fleeting. Do something about her will tomorrow, thought Mrs. Ivy, never dreaming that her death from entirely natural causes was less than four weeks away. Not something so radical that it could be fought with success, but a measure so that they would know she had not been an utter fool.

She looked at Roger in his basket, and Roger, who did not quote spiteful poetry about her or criticize her choice of liquor, gazed sparklingly back out of his foolish and eyebrowy hair.

# Chapter

# Two

This, the moment of her arrival to take over the graveyard shift at the Emergency Animal Clinic, was what young Deb Kingsley dreaded about her new job.

Under normal circumstances it would have been only a few steps from her car to the rear entrance of the long, low building. Now, because of the havoc wrought by burst pipes in mid-December, parking was at the far side of the asphalt apron, with a consequent run through the bitter cold, a picking of her way over wooden planks between piles of sand, a wait of seconds after she had knocked.

There were brilliant arc lights here as well as at the front, but on nights like this, with a wind rushing off the ocean to wrestle in the bare tree branches, they made matters worse; the asphalt came alive with slender black images that might have concealed a sly noose to wriggle up one of her ankles and send her crashing. She made it safely, called "Deb" to the automatic query from within, and stood shivering and listening to a perfunctory barking from the back ward until the door opened.

"Did you know you were giving the clinic ten free minutes?" inquired Belinda Grace.

"I nearly gave the clinic a new patient while I was out shopping this afternoon, too," said Deb. "Honestly, people who let their dogs run loose ought to put in a day's work here."

Head scarf pocketed, she took off her coat and hung it in her locker along with the change of clothes required of all attendants; animals, especially frightened puppies, could misbehave without warning. Then she followed the other girl into the main clinic.

Something about Belinda Grace puzzled them all. She was the oldest of the three attendants, mid-twenties at least, and although she was friendly, and calm and good with animals, she seemed subtly alien to the business of taking temperatures, washing down and disinfecting cages, collecting used bedding, mostly old towels and pieces of blanket, some provided by clients and some by the clinic, for the washing machine.

It was a low-wage job, of interest chiefly to veterinary-school aspirants, and there was an extremely unminimum-wage quality about Belinda Grace. Not her car, which was long out of the showroom, nor, as they had to conform to a dress code of slacks and smocks in a selected range of colors (brown was professional, blue cooperative, yellow cheerful, while white and green were too surgical and red too exciting, as witness the extensive use of it in restaurant decor) her clothes.

Something about the poise of her silky, light brown head, or her eyes? Whatever it was, she appeared to Deb like someone who could stipulate the furnishing of her office and commandeer the services of at least a typist at will.

Lastly and most intriguingly, she had asked the receptionist-bookkeeper, Mrs. Espinosa, and Deb and the stylish black Hilda to say, if a man telephoned for her, that they had no Belinda Grace working there. Not such an unusual request in itself—every girl got saddled now and then with a nuisance who wouldn't take no for an answer—but it wasn't usual to look sick about it.

In the big brilliant room with its cabinets and two steel examining tables, Belinda gave a fast recap of the caged animals dealt with during her shift, including a nine-year-old Pekingese who had had windpipe surgery an hour earlier. "And Dr. Cooper wants to be waked if the malamute in the back ward starts turning in circles."

She picked her coat up from a wheeled stool. "There's a Mr. Warner coming in with a cat in about fifteen minutes. I've started a card, it's over there on the counter. Shall I lock the front, or will you?"

This was a ritual that took place at midnight, and as the wall clock still showed five minutes of, Deb said that she would. "Has it been very busy? You look awfully tired."

"I'm dead," said Belinda, and then in a fast, knock-on-wood fashion, "Well, not quite. In one short period of time we had two hit dogs—one died between reception and here—and a man who got so furious at the wording on the release form that Dr. Cooper told him to either stop crossing things out or take his dog and go home."

She pushed a lock of hair back from her forehead; under the ruthless fluorescent lighting it caught shimmers of lilac and gold. "Which he did, and I am about to too. Good-night."

The Emergency Animal Clinic was the flourishing enterprise of fourteen North Shore veterinarians, into whose nine-to-five practices flowed the cats, dogs, and occasional exotics brought in from a wide area and dealt with during the intervening hours by the director and three staff doctors whom they had hired.

Although its average overnight tenancy was twelve, the clinic treated and dismissed many more animals than that in its day/night span, and had a capacity for forty. This was put to strain on long holiday weekends and in January, when pets unwisely bestowed on young children at Christmas were brought in with dangerous substances ingested, tails or necks infected where rubber bands had bitten deeply in, injuries from being dropped.

On one well-remembered Labor Day there had been overflow patients in the storage room, both washrooms, and the lounge with its refrigerator and coffeemaker. It was during this time that the usually genial Dr. Kitsch, who ran the clinic, had been overheard to say in a voice of steel, "I—don't—see—ducks."

With the hands of the wall clock straight up, Deb Kingsley walked through the smaller examining room. Ahead of her, the reception area was bright, to her left the office darkened so that from there the night attendant could see with undazzled eyes who stood outside the windowed door.

Although there had been only a searching wind ten minutes earlier, it was one of the surprises of working in an otherwise windowless facility that the square of glass was now half masked with rain. Deb locked the door, went back to the storage room for a strip of rug to put down in front of it, and returned to the main clinic.

In view of the fact that they were there in the first place, the recumbent animals had to be checked with frequency to see if they responded to the drawing of something hard across their cage fronts. Deb used a ballpoint pen. The Pekingese with the catheter for drip solution still strapped to its foreleg gave her a sleepy blink. She proceeded to the back ward.

Here were the runs for the bigger breeds, tonight the malamute, who was not turning in circles, and an English sheep dog with a woebegone face. Here too were the pair of resident blood-donor cats, currently a tortoiseshell and a yellow barred with marmalade. Deb had felt a pang about them until Hilda told her that they didn't fulfill their function more than two or three times. One of the attendants or the cleaning staff adopted or found other homes for them, and a replacement pair of cats escaped their fate at the shelter.

She went back to her post to begin the nightly restocking of drugs, drip sets, needles, gauze, tape. According to Belinda, the man with the cat, Mr. Warner, was almost due, unless he

*10*

had changed his mind because of the rain. People were generally good about calling ahead, not so punctilious about canceling.

Shudder at this job though some of her friends might, and it was certainly not for the queasy, there were fringe benefits. In less than three weeks she had automatically picked up a few snippets of veterinary information, and relatives who had dismissed her as just another amiable nineteen-year-old listened to her with respect and were almost slavishly grateful when she gave their pets parvo and DHL shots. She hadn't had to buy her own gas since coming to work here.

On the other hand, although any problems a cat had were usually solved on the spot, Deb had a new awareness of what even glancing contact with a wheel or bumper could do to a dog. That afternoon, as she drove home along River Road with groceries for her mother in the back seat, only fast reflexes and the Mustang's relined brakes had brought her to a jolting, swerving stop inches from hitting a low-slung fawn dog crossing directly in front of her with a curious rocking-horse gait.

The long screech of her brakes tore through the cold air. The dog paused at a stretch of dry stone wall, vandalized in places, to gaze victoriously over its shoulder, not at the car but at a man just inside a narrow lilac-bordered driveway. Deb didn't know who lived there but she knew the house—very old, its shingles almost black—because every year summer people in careful hats set up their easels across the way.

From the ragged length of rope he was stuffing into a coat pocket, the man was the responsible party. The dog had vanished. Deb, shaken with reaction from the near miss, was furious.

She wound down her window. "I work at the emergency clinic," she called, "and I hope I don't have to put that dog out of its misery some night soon."

"Sorry." It was a perfunctory shout back, with a shielding hand coming up as massed clouds in the west parted and icy lemon rays came flaring at him. "She took off after a rabbit."

*She.* To someone in the fresh habit of noticing all dogs in detail, it was so ridiculous that Deb's good humor was in large part restored. "Don't expect a whole lot of puppies," she advised, and drove off.

Twelve-ten came and went, and so did a second check of the cages. The telephone stayed eerily silent. People looking out their wet windows, thought Deb, Mr. Warner among them, and deciding that what had seemed like an emergency could wait until morning.

The door buzzer sounded.

Although it echoed everywhere in the clinic, even the storage room, Deb did not go immediately to summon Dr. Cooper, who might have slept through it; twice in her tenure it had meant a lost motorist who needed directions and another who wanted to use the phone.

Instead, she went into the receptionist's office, peered through at the shape of a man's hat over the glint of glasses, and proceeded into the brightness of the reception area, punctuated with vinyl chairs and couches, a few plants, a stand with magazines.

"Mr. Warner?" Loudly, to carry against the wind and rain, into the small device beside the door.

Water planed across the glass, the hat brim nodded to reinforce a dim yes.

"Just a minute, the doctor will be right with you."

Deb smiled apologetically, turned, retraced her steps with speed. This was a rule since an incident in September, which nobody wanted to talk about; all she could gather was that a spaced-out boy in search of drugs had turned rape-minded instead. Ever since, female attendants had been required to alert the vet on duty before admitting anyone after midnight.

The room equipped with a daybed opened off Dr. Kitsch's office. All was quiet behind the closed door; Dr. Cooper had indeed slept through the buzzer. Deb knocked briskly and said to the instant creak of springs, "There's a client here with a cat, Doctor. He phoned ahead."

Sound of feet hitting the floor, sensible tile everywhere

except for the hoseable concrete in the runs. "Okay, let him in."

When they had been roused from sleep, all the vets tended to step into the adjoining bath and splash cold water on their faces and run a brush over their hair before donning the white laboratory coat that hung on an inside hook. All of eighty or ninety seconds, perhaps.

But it was pouring and blowing, and both cat and owner would be increasingly unhappy. Deb Kingsley sped back through the black-and-white brilliance to the front door, turned the lock, slid the security bolt, and said, "I'm sorry I had to keep you wait—" to the last face she ever saw.

# Chapter
# Three

"No, you may not," said Hattie Callahan to the dog who was riveting his gaze on hers like a hairy little hypnotist. "I can't trust you any more."

Charlotte Ivy had been in her grave for over two months, but it was only within the last week or so that Hattie had brought herself to address Roger with any real familiarity. To criticize him to his face had seemed as unthinkable at first as juggling a Ming vase on a stone floor.

It was because of him, her legal charge, that Charlotte's house was now hers, because of him that a trust set up under the terms of Charlotte's will would pay her twenty-five thousand dollars a year as long as he lived. And he was approximately one and a half.

The astonishment was only now wearing off. At sixty-two, smallish, never a sylph, gray-haired but as pink and white as a girl despite the decades of nursing toil, Hattie had matter-of-factly expected to inherit something from the older cousin whose frequent chauffeur she had been since the onset of deafness. As Charlotte had already bestowed the silver-gray Buick she no longer felt fully competent to drive, five thousand would have appeared the outside limit, with possibly a piece of keepsake jewelry thrown in. The young Aintrees were much closer to her by blood.

Moreover, they were confident, good-looking people, and Charlotte, something of a beauty herself all her life, had prized physical attractiveness as other people prized integrity or reliability. Hattie was—she cast honesty about in her mind—wholesome, and totally sure of herself only with her cats and in her kitchen, where she produced surprising meals instead of the New England boiled dinners that might have been expected of her.

What had happened, then? Bernard Odom, Charlotte's friend as well as her lawyer, almost certainly knew, although he wasn't telling. There had been a trace of dry fun in his voice when, inviting Hattie to his office to learn the contents of the will, he had said, "It would be appropriate for the dog to come too."

Because she had brought Roger home with her when Charlotte was sped to the hospital with chest pains. The others would be coming and going or maintaining vigils; besides, she was the background kind of relative who was expected to take on such tasks. Upon Charlotte's death, the Aintrees left Hattie firmly in a quandary. Laurence's wife was allergic to dogs; the Farrises owned a German shepherd, which they said complacently would make mincemeat of Roger; Donald's landlady did not allow pets.

Apart from sharing her cousin's erstwhile aversion to dogs in general, Hattie already had one animal in her very small house, a large white cat, which was the current one of many bestowed on her as kittens by grateful patients. (Donald had once said with a pondering air, "I wonder what they'd give you if they bore a grudge?")

*15*

Still, because it wasn't likely that Roger would be claimed twice, Hattie saw it her duty to Charlotte to make an effort to find him another home before returning him to the animal shelter. She introduced him to Whitey, who at the other end of the spectrum would have been christened Blackie, and was amazed to discover that he thought, unrequitedly, that he had found a playmate.

That was the state of affairs on the morning when she arrived at Bernard Odom's office with her leashed companion, early because her watch was fast. Although the lawyer had seen Roger at the house, he made an interested circle of inspection before sitting down at his desk to make small talk about the extreme cold. Perhaps because his head was bent as he reviewed the document in readiness, something emerged sounding like "the advisability of a small fur for Roger," but that couldn't have been.

Presently, Laurence and Donald and Nan Aintree Farris showed no surprise at finding their aunt's dog among the audience; they knew that Hattie shared close quarters with a cat. Having made it clear that he was to be no part of their lives, they were cordial to Roger, and he was cordial back.

"Mrs. Ivy's will is essentially a very simple one," began Odom, "so I'll get right into it without the preliminaries, as you'll all receive a copy. 'To my nephew, Laurence J. Aintree . . .' "

The sum of five thousand dollars plus one-third of Charlotte's jewelry, which was considerable. Hattie, listening as these same words were repeated in the case of Nan and Donald, did not understand what she was hearing, was unaware of the freeze that had set in around her. There, she thought, went any hope of a small pin on which she had had an innocently covetous eye, a rose made of gold with a small pearl at its heart.

" 'To my cousin, and loyal chauffeur, Harriet E. Callahan, 29 Front Street, Pippin, Massachusetts . . .' "

At first, because of its very unlikelihood, the bomb appeared to be a dud. It took three or four seconds to explode without sound.

Everybody stared at Roger. After his wagging salutation to the Aintrees he had sat smartly, head up and ears alert, as ready as anyone else for the proceedings to begin. Gradually, because of the inordinate length of his spine, he began a slump. Whiskers down, contemplating the gray broadloom in a kind of vacant reverie, he looked like a dog just informed that he had been wiped out in the market.

"When——" Laurence had to clear his throat and begin again. "When is this will dated?"

A trace of breathlessness entered the office. "The ninth of October. All previous wills, although in fact there was only one, are disclaimed," said Odom. "There is also the usual penalty for any legatee disputing the terms. The provisions of the trust are somewhat lengthy, and you may want to examine those at your leisure, but it's all in order."

Hattie, sitting wrapped in shock as well as her tweed coat, was nevertheless aware that those dark-lashed, grayed-blue gazes were now focused upon her, the distant, casually familiar relative from whom—she was always aware of it in their ranked presence—it would be suitable to buy eggs.

Didn't this situation have a considerable hazard built into it?

"Should anything happen to prevent Miss Callahan from carrying out her duties as guardian," Odom's reassuring flick of a glance suggested nothing more serious than a broken leg, "another guardian will be appointed by the trustees. Should anything of a . . . startling nature befall Roger in his prime, so to speak, there will be a full-scale investigation, for which funds are to be sequestered."

He smiled impartially around the office. To Hattie, who had often seen him relaxed in her cousin's living room with tea or Scotch, depending on the hour, the smile had an element of blandness. "Mere technicalities. I'm sure we all, as Mrs. Ivy so clearly did, wish Roger a long and happy life. Would you," he bent courteously toward Nan in her sudden attack of hiccups, "care for a glass of water?"

That had been in November. On this January night there was a wind rising, which meant, to anyone who had lived in Pippin as long as Hattie, that rain was not far behind it. Up until four hours ago she would have let the importunate Roger into the utility room, where he could push his way through the flap door and out into the fenced area in the hollow corner of the house.

Of these innovations, completed only two weeks before Charlotte's death, Laurence had said with a lift of his eyebrows, "You're going to see a change in your heating bill."

"I know," said Mrs. Ivy.

But this afternoon, the day of the week when she donated her services to the free blood-pressure clinic, Hattie had come home in the early dark to find the house empty except for Whitey, giving her a rough trill of greeting from the top of the refrigerator.

Had the dog door somehow jammed, leaving Roger stranded in his run? No; it swung easily at the touch of her foot.

Fright, only inches away from panic, had settled over her like a drop cloth. Roger was now not only a part of her daily life, he was a large part of her future. There were even times—as he sat staring captivatedly at Whitey, not trembling so much as a whisker, or maintained a nose-down vigil in front of the chair under which he thought his quarry was hiding, while the cat sauntered scornfully up behind him and began to bat at his tail—when she felt something like a reluctant affection.

She went outside with a flashlight, dreading the sight of a stiff little body. The run under the maple tree was empty, with, near one corner, evidence that he had dug his way under the chain-link fencing.

How many hours ago? What were the chances that she would ever see him again? It would be the end of the trust. She—

*18*

That was when, at the front of the house and as if he had been observing it from a careful distance, Roger barked.

And here he was, demanding to go out again. He had seemed quite happy to be back from his unprecedented roaming; still, he could not be allowed access to his new escape hatch. Hattie said coaxingly, "Where's Whitey?" but Roger only cast the briefest of glances at the dining room chair where the cat reposed, settled his haunches more firmly, and resumed his beady and drill-like stare.

It would have to be his leash, in spite of the wind, which was now pounding out of the east. Hattie, going resignedly for her coat, wondered what had suddenly prompted him to dig in the first place. He was very law-abiding, for a dog, and it couldn't be a female in the neighborhood because Charlotte had had him neutered.

The thaw, probably; the discovery that after weeks of snowy cold the ground was almost spongy. Or maybe Charlotte had christened the completed run with a bone, and he had all at once remembered it.

He was unrepentant when Hattie conducted him to the fence for a scolding by flashlight; he simply sniffed alertly at the grass and disturbed earth, as though on the track of an interloper, and then indicated his wish to go elsewhere. Hattie let him tug her, shivering in the wind. She couldn't look forward to endless, frigid walks. She would have to have the fence electrified.

The Aintrees mustn't find out about this.

Hattie could not have explained her absolute conviction that secrecy about Roger's unchaperoned wandering was essential. It certainly wasn't because they treasured him as a living memento of Charlotte, or would worry that in the event of his loss she would be left with only the house and no way to maintain it on her tiny fixed income. Whereas if she were careful with the trust during his lifetime . . .

After their first thunderstruck reaction they had all, Laurence and Nan and Donald, been civility itself over the will. A wordless communion had passed among them about its dating: Laurence glancing quickly at his sister, who lifted her chin a little as she met his eyes, Donald surveying them both. But perhaps—two seconds had passed too quickly to be sure— they were only measuring each other for shock.

Hattie, admiring their aplomb once Nan had gotten over her hiccups, had had to remind herself that it was not as if they were so situated to have banked desperately on immediate inheritance. Laurence did well in his brokerage house, and in addition had married a cashmere-and-pearls girl, only daughter of a wealthy shipbuilder. It had to be conceded that this was sometimes only the guarantee of a wife with expensive tastes, but she looked to Hattie like the kind of daughter whose parents would not dare do anything fickle with their money.

Donald. . . . But he was footloose and able-bodied, and besides, Hattie had met him a few weeks ago coming out of the stationery store with a package identified at one end as eight-and-a-half-by-eleven Canary under his arm. He wasn't supposed to have been near his typewriter for long months, and he had said rapidly, "Don't tell anybody."

For fear of having progress reports demanded of him, Hattie supposed. She had read and liked his mildly successful book two years ago, the copy tendered out of good will and the pride of first publication, although he had diplomatically not asked her for a reaction. But then, she was sure, they all thought of her as curling up with the *Old Farmer's Almanac* if she curled up with anything at all.

Oddly, her very shrewdness as to the Aintree view of her blinded Hattie to the fact that she was not the only person in the world or even in Pippin whose life was not what it seemed on the surface. She simply knew as she returned to the warmth of the house that she would keep quiet about Roger's escape.

It was well after midnight when, Roger in his basket in the

darkened downstairs, Whitey installed at the foot of her bed, Hattie turned out the light in the room that had been Charlotte's.

Deborah Kingsley's nineteen years had been over for half an hour. Belinda Grace's hard-won healing was shortly to be ripped open.

# Chapter
# Four

"This bitch needs help to whelp!" cried the distraught woman in front of the emergency clinic. It was the second time she had unloosed her bizarre collection of syllables, and now she ran the few steps to her station wagon and wrenched open its rear door.

Officer Pearl, mutely commanded, advanced and peered inside. The Dalmation stretched on a blanket certainly did not look happy.

"*Please*," said the woman changing to an imploring tone. "Just tell the vet on duty that it's Peg's Domino."

By now, photographs had been taken and a blanketed and stretcher-strapped Deborah Kingsley borne away. The coroner's car had departed along with the ambulance, leaving only the patrol car and Lieutenant Charles Hallam's. There had never been a great swarm of experts and equipment; the incorporated township of Pippin did not have the manpower to deploy them in a case where common sense said the exercise would be only that.

The girl had been shot in the chest twice at very close range, the second time according to the coroner, as she was falling. From the high flawless polish of the reception area floor, the killer had not stepped anywhere but on the protective strip of carpeting, partly covered by the body, which had been rolled up, bagged, tagged, and carried off.

Still, the premises had to be searched for the off-chance weapon and pair of wet shoes, and while that was going on Officer Pearl had been detailed to stand outside and inform any comers that there had been an accident and the clinic was temporarily closed.

Nearly half an hour had passed. Pearl pressed the buzzer. He said when the door opened a crack and Hallam's dark gray eye came into view, surprisingly wintry, "There's a Dalmation out here, name of Domino, in some kind of trouble. The owner says the vet—"

"Peg's Domino." The vet, appearing in slice form, looked like a jaunty boy with his pointed face and headful of chestnut curls. Pearl, not knowing that Dr. Vincent Cooper was highly respected for his placing of steel pins in messy fractures, would not have entrusted an alley cat to him. "She's a valuable show animal and overdue for a litter, Lieutenant. Surely there can't be any harm in receiving her at the back."

"Oh, receive her at the back by all means," said Hallam, and Officer Pearl, startled all over again at the undoubted bite in the usually calm and easy voice, went back to advise the woman beside the station wagon. She slammed herself in behind the wheel at once, and for all her distraction remembered whose eye was on her; she flicked on her turn signal before disappearing around the end of the building.

Pearl, returning to his post, wondered what was getting to Hallam in this marked fashion. A young girl blasted into eternity was depressing, certainly, but at thirty-six and a veteran in Homicide, Hallam was used to riding with things like that.

Was it possible—Pearl was as gossipy to himself as a whole quilting bee—that the girl somehow reminded him of his wife?

\*     \*     \*

23

A framed sign on the far wall of the reception area did not thank Hallam for not smoking; it forbade him. He didn't consider that it applied under the circumstances, and, after casting an eye around the spotless and hygienic surroundings, deposited the match in the earth around a great and eager plant suspended from the ceiling by macrame.

From the back of the clinic and progressing inward came a woman's excited voice and Cooper's soothing tones. Closer at hand, in the receptionist's office behind its bulletproof glass, the uniformed sergeant, Uffi, was methodically completing the sweep that would almost certainly be fruitless. Even granted a motive for wanting a new employee out of the way, Cooper wouldn't be fool enough to commit murder in his own professional territory and at a time when he was alone with her.

A house of this square footage would have been an undertaking to search, a two-man job if it weren't to take all night. The clinic, in spite of its drawers and cabinets and lockers, its X-ray and drug and storage rooms, was essentially a bare and sterile place; even in the lounge, the sole place for relaxation, the chairs were cushionless, cup-shaped plastic. Failing wet shoes hidden in the receptionist's desk, or an arm like an outfielder's, Cooper's statement was the truth.

He had been waked by Deborah Kingsley at shortly after midnight, he said, with the information that a client, expected, had arrived with a cat. He had told her to let the man in, given himself a fast wake-up with cold water, brushed his hair (his work cut out for him right there, thought Hallam unkindly), and was putting on his laboratory coat when he heard a shot and, so close that it might have been an echo, a second, followed by the closing of the door. He estimated the time elapsed from the girl's knock to be a little over a minute.

When he reached the front, Deborah Kingsley lay on her face with blood on the back of her smock. Cooper's first act had been to yank the door open on an empty parking lot—no taillights, no sound audible above the rain; his second, instinctive because of his training, to turn the girl over and make an attempt at resuscitation. Then he had called the police.

Hallam was inclined to believe all of this except for the speed with which Cooper said he had reached the reception area. Unless the life of a family member could be presumed at stake, people taken by surprise did not usually respond that way. There was much more apt to be a delayed recognition of what the sound represented, a perfectly natural "Will *I* get shot if I go out there?"—at least a temporary weighing of the situation.

Hallam thought it probable that, instead of the headlong dash implied, Cooper had waited to make sure that the door closing had not been a decoy to flush out any other presence in the building. It wasn't important. The girl had died instantly, and with a car engine left running, a single minute would have sufficed for disappearance.

"Nothing," said Uffi unnecessarily, emerging from the receptionist's office. He grimaced toward the rear. "Nice little surprise in the freezer, though, a dead dog in a bag."

On the stretch of counter that also held a stack of release forms, a chained pen, and a display of the credit cards accepted, the telephone rang.

By prearrangement with Cooper, Hallam picked it up with a certain tension (How sure could the killer be that his victim was dead? There were astonishing flukes with guns.) and said a neutral, "Emergency Clinic."

"Oh, I'm so sorry to bother you again." It was a dithery female voice that sounded as if it had a good deal to apologize for. "I couldn't sleep, wondering if my little Jade Boy has come out of the anaesthetic yet."

Jade Boy. Hallam's expression hardened. He said curtly, "Yes, he has," presuming the object of inquiry to be the caged dog in the big bright room who had given him a bulbous stare on his swift initial tour of the premises.

"I'm so glad. Did you find a button as well as the needle and thread? Because it occurred to me—"

"The doctor is busy right now, but I'll tell him you called," interrupted Hallam. "Good-night. . . . If it rings again in the next thirty seconds," he said to Uffi, "you answer it."

It was the first incoming call since their arrival on the scene. Hallam had telephoned the Kingsleys, making what often proved to be a form of therapy out of the need for a list of their daughter's associates and her activities of the past few days and telling them that he would be there in about an hour.

Then, pausing only to break the connection, he had dialed the number written after Warner, John, and the address on the card in a handwriting that Cooper said belonged to the attendant on the previous shift, Belinda Grace.

Predictably, he had been answered by an irate old voice, obviously roused from sleep, which informed him that he had the Giordano residence and that at that time of night it was a pity people couldn't take the trouble to be more careful.

In another flurry of telephone activity, the boy involved in the previous incident at the clinic had been picked up for questioning, but so far he didn't look likely. It had been decided on a number of heads that the clinic could remain open, and another attendant was on her way with the agreement that Officer Pearl would take up his station inside.

"You may think we're heartless, Lieutenant," said Dr. Cooper, "but this is an emergency facility and people do come from a radius of thirty miles and more. Besides, we have animals here who simply can't be left."

Hallam, whose marriage had been scratched and mewed and barked and chewed to pieces while the dew was still on it, could have left them with a will. He spoke briefly to Sergeant Uffi and let himself out into the rain.

The house in which Belinda Grace lived was wrapped tonight in a roar of wind that carried the faint rhythmic crash of solider water. It had been built in the 1790s by twin sea captains for their brides, and although Hallam had never been inside, he knew that originally the staircase had divided identical living quarters, with the only common room a long kitchen stretching along the back.

26

It had since been remodeled into apartments, two up and two down. Hallam, examining the name plates in the partially enclosed overhang outside the graceful front door, had to look hard for his quarry. D. Aintree, P. L. Coe, H. Calvacaressi . . . here she was, a lightly penciled-in B. Grace above Z. Zulalian.

According to the pattern of buttons, that would be the top floor left, where a lighted rectangular window broke the dark. Even at a little after one o'clock, it was what Hallam had banked on: that someone returning from that particular eight-hour shift would have a meal of sorts before commencing the going-to-bed process.

(Although Sue had done any face-creaming or hair-pinning when he wasn't home; with her, it had been a matter of a fast shower and energetic teeth-brushing.)

Hallam yanked that recollection up and tossed it aside like a weed from an increasingly disciplined garden. He had pressed the button beside Zulalian/Grace, and now the door buzzed back at him and he entered a small, warm, softly lit hall. Shadowy spaces surrounding the stairwell; directly ahead, un-carpeted either out of thrift or pride in the shining old wood, a flight of steps.

At the top stood an obviously startled girl in a housecoat; that confident door release had been for someone she expected.

"Miss Grace? Lieutenant Hallam, police." He was climbing as he spoke. "I realize that it's late, but I'd like to talk to you for a few minutes if I may."

She checked a movement of recoil; the polished pale green quilting that hung straight from her shoulders to the tips of her slippers swayed a little. "About what?"

Hallam reached the landing. "Deborah Kingsley," he said, consciously gentle because although no one liked a small-hours visit from the police this girl's expression had something in it much deeper than automatic alarm. "Could we—"

And at the same time she said in a tone of civil wonder, "Shouldn't you be showing me some kind of identification?"

Perfectly right and proper; the fault was his. Still, delving inside his wet raincoat, Hallam felt a prickle of antagonism. When Belinda Grace dropped her gaze to inspect his wallet card, he did some cool close-up inspecting of his own.

The hair in feathery points, not the gold it had looked from the foot of the stairs with the light behind her, but the color of milky tea. Dark brows and lashes, a clean satiny polish to the lightly hollowed cheeks. That, together with a powdery scent, suggested that she was just out of a bath.

And nobody could take this long over his credentials; she was bracing herself while he stood there like a carpet salesman who had presented samples. Hallam flipped his wallet closed. He said, "Deborah Kingsley was shot and killed at just after midnight. As you saw her last, and took what we've found to be a phony call about a cat, you may be able to help us."

"*Deb?*" Belinda Grace caught a horrified breath and stared at him with something close to fierceness. "Oh, God, and it was the back parking lot that she was afraid of, she always ran. . . . I don't know what I can tell you, I scarcely knew her, but come in."

For someone scarcely known, it had been a violent reaction, thought Hallam, but then her manner had been a little odd all along. He followed her down a carpeted hall to a partly open door, which she pushed wider on a room that seemed to be mainly honey color and black, and then closed behind him.

"I don't think it was anything specific about the parking lot," she said, anticipating his question and making an unstrung gesture at a chair, "it was just the way some people feel about closets, that there might be somebody in there." She added with reluctant courtesy, "I can take your coat, if you like."

"No, thanks. What time did this Mr. Warner call?"

"About a quarter of twelve, because I'd just finished making out a record card when Deb arrived, early, ten minutes of."

"Was that usual?"

A date cut short by a quarrel came automatically to mind, but Belinda Grace said, "Yes. She was always at least a few

*28*

minutes ahead of time. She wanted to become a veterinarian and she was very," a glance down at the tightly joined hands in her quilted lap, "eager."

It was a terrible word to apply to a stilled young girl with blood on her back.

"Did she ever mention boyfriends?"

"Not to me. It was a strictly coming-and-going thing, just hello and a fast running over of the cases on my shift and good-bye."

Back to that set-up telephone call. "What exactly did Warner say?"

"That his cat was having fits, literal ones, and he'd bring it in in half an hour or less."

(Sue, tirelessly and ruthlessly tenderhearted, had brought home a kitten with ringworm, which—"Oh, honey, leave him there, the poor thing's just gotten to sleep. Can't you sit in another chair for tonight?"—had transferred itself to Hallam at speed.)

He contained a ripple of aversion. "Anything in particular about his voice?"

The telephone rang with the eruptive urgency of all telephones after a certain hour. Hallam, watching Belinda Grace cross the room to pick up the receiver, wondered if the seascapes tacked up here and there on the honey-painted walls were hers: bold green and blue and white-slashed gray, executed with the reckless confidence of a child.

Or were they the work of Z. Zulalian, for whose first name there weren't a great many choices? Zachary? Zebediah? Zorro?

"Hello? Oh . . . well, no tearing hurry. Could I call you back? . . . No. Far from it."

There was a tinge of bitterness or despair in that. She hung up without another word and buried her hands in her pockets; Hallam thought he knew why. "The voice," she said after seconds of blank contemplation. "No. I don't think I'd recognize it again, if that's what you mean."

She was staying implacably on her feet, and Hallam rose

to his; time, in any case, that he got to the Kingsleys'. He uttered the formula about letting him know if she remembered anything that might be useful to the investigation, said good-night, resisted an impulse to step loudly on the first few stair treads and then steal back to put his ear to the door, and departed.

As he got into his car, he tried to imagine that girl doing what amounted to zoo chores, and could not.


"Kieran," Mrs. Kingsley was saying exhaustedly to her young son, "why don't you go to bed? There's school—"

She stopped, aghast, at the mindless repetition of what she had had to tell him so often. As if he would go to school on this particular day, even if it were not now Saturday.

Fourteen, already tall and rangy, frequently at loggerheads with his older sister, Kieran was now trying to make up for it by wild suggestions as to enemies. He had already put forward a friend of Deborah's with whom there had been a short war over a visiting college boy last summer, and the son of a neighbor who had a crush on her although Deb had defined him darkly as a wimp.

His parents eyed him tiredly, too emotionally spent to tell him that all this was nonsense, but his pallor and his big-knuckled hands were pitiable and Sergeant Uffi regarded him with kindness. He paid attention when Kieran said desperately, "Deb really chewed some guy out this afternoon."

They all looked at him, his father and mother with a faint return of interest. It was Uffi who said encouragingly, "What was that about?"

The usually glib Kieran was semistrangled by sudden death, permanent loss, heated accusations that couldn't be taken back, words going into a notebook to be filed somewhere. "This dog ran out in front of her car, and she nearly hit it. I mean it wasn't just a stray dog, there was a guy with it."

Everybody waited for the end of the story. Kieran stared at

30

his hands and said on a descending scale, "He might have gotten mad about that."

There was a short silence, which Uffi put an end to by saying, "Well, we'll keep that in mind."

How they would keep it in mind without learning where the near accident had taken place he did not specify, and nobody asked him.

.

# Chapter
# Five

For a matter of moments after the fair-haired detective had
followed her into her apartment, tall in his raincoat, Belinda
had considered walking straight to the telephone, flipping the
Pippin directory open to the K's, asking a single brutal question
of whatever Kingsley she got. There couldn't be that many.

Now it came down to shock, sorrow over a life pocketed
as swiftly as a trinket from the five-and-ten, a shivering reaction
from the very center of her. She couldn't even make a cup of
hot, strong tea with a jigger of rum poured tremblingly into it
because that would only complete the damage.

November. A night very much like this, the time approximately the same. But the beginning of it had been much earlier.
March.

She had been boundlessly happy returning that late afternoon
to the apartment that wasn't quite on Beacon Hill. Not even
the fact that the self-service elevator was out of order again
could irritate her. Just as there were last-straw moments, there

were times, admittedly rarer, when relatively simple things like a new coat, new job, two blue Oriental rugs bought at an auction over the weekend, came together to form a perfect felicity.

The frequent nonperformance of the elevator kept all the tenants in training. Although Belinda was burdened with a bag of groceries, she was only a little breathless when she reached the fourth floor and saw the man sitting on the stairs that led to the roof.

"Boy" was the term that came to mind first, because of the blond hair that was silkily too long, the corduroys, the enormous backpack at his feet. His eyes, hollowed as if from fatigue or hunger, were not that young. His mouth had a firm angelic cut.

"If you're looking for the Bests, they're out of town," said Belinda, apologetic in view of her own cloudless horizon. "They won't be back until next week."

It was clearly the blow that the backpack had indicated. He had gotten to his feet; he said, "My name is Norman Comstock," and added protestingly, "I met the Bests in New Orleans last month and they said to be sure and look them up if I got to Boston."

And he had actually taken that at face value. He caught Belinda's silent marveling. "They did seem to mean it, and if they didn't," surprising little tweak of the mouth corners, "people ought to be taught a lesson."

Belinda was inclined to agree with him. It must feel quite lordly to issue those invitations at a safe distance from home, with the implication that they always wore their festive holiday faces, a guest room was constantly at the ready, meals and entertaining in general no problem whatsoever.

"Do you have a number where I can reach them, just to say hello and that I did get to Boston? I'll pay, of course," said Norman Comstock.

Belinda's left arm was beginning to ache from the groceries. She did have a number for the Bests, whom she knew slightly from the elevator, the stairs, and the small market in the next block, although she couldn't remember the contingency reason for which they had given it to her. And who was she to say that they had not been totally sincere, and would blame her if Norman Comstock backpacked his way permanently out of their lives?

The upshot was that she let him into her apartment, aware that if someone else had described this action to her she would have considered it madness. But he was—different, somehow.

While she searched for the telephone number, and after he had said, "I love your rugs, it must be like living on a lake," he told her about himself. He came from Pennsylvania, where his parents had a thriving furniture business into which they had been trying to press him ever since he left college. He hated furniture, he wrote poetry and had actually had some of it published, had taken to the road to find a place into which he could fit and a bearable occupation to support him.

He did, apparently, a little of everything. He could cook, play jazz piano, house paint, do auto repairs. His voice had stood him in good stead too; more than once during his winter wanderings he had filled in for a local disc jockey struck down by flu or laryngitis.

And he did indeed sound mellifluous when he said, "Mrs. Best? Norman Comstock. Do you remember me from New Orleans?" As he listened, his eyebrows were up at Belinda, suggesting a complicity, which for some reason she didn't mind. "Well, as a matter of fact, I haven't. . . . Oh, but I couldn't take advant—no, I won't do that, but I'd be enormously grateful if I could unroll my sleeping bag on your floor just for tonight. I'll find a room of some kind tomorrow. How is Mr. Best? . . ."

As arranged, Mrs. Best called the building superintendent from her mother's house in New Jersey, and in a short time Norman had harbor for the night. It wasn't really that much of a risk, thought Belinda after her first bemusement. The Bests had obviously seen enough of him in New Orleans to like and trust him; anything of great value would have been put in the bank; most tellingly, he was known to be there.

In the same bemusement she allowed herself to be taken to dinner—"Pizza," said Norman after a candid consultation with his wallet and a folder containing a single traveler's check—but, in an establishing of their future relationship, insisted on buying the red wine.

Perhaps because of her current gaiety, she felt as easy with him as if he were a cousin, often talked about but just now met. She told him a little about the new magazine where she had been hired as associate editor—"That's not as impressive as it sounds, there are quite a few of us"—and that she had been living in the apartment only since the first of the year, moving there from a tiny warren of a place off Dartmouth Street. For fresh air and an occasional glimpse of country, there was her parents' house in Bedlington.

"I still drive down every few weekends. People look at me as if I'm trailing an umbilical cord eighteen miles long, but they're very good company."

It was understood that Norman would hunt for a room in the immediate neighborhood, and by the end of the next day he had found one. A job was not as easily come by, as he was not yet prepared to face being a dishwasher, and when Belinda discovered that he was living mainly on packaged custard, she lent him fifty dollars and fell into the habit of having him to dinner once a week. There was no panoply involved; she simply made three times as much of whatever she would have prepared for herself because he ate as if he were still growing.

He dropped into a slot of her life that she hadn't known existed. He was interesting, a little touching in a way she couldn't define, and companionable even after the night when, surprising something speculative in his manner, she said forthrightly, "If you're looking for a bedmate, Norman, you'll have to look elsewhere," because the mere idea was so unnatural, so close to the incestuous, as to be put to death right away.

After that first evening, Norman mentioned his poetry only

once, when he remarked lightly that he would have to write something about her blue rugs and mirrors. Belinda's apartment did contain a number of mirrors, not for purposes of preening but because to her they were a summing up of water and light. There, however, the matter seemed to drop.

Through the Bests, he got a job in a large greeting-card company, but although presumably he met people there, he was never far out of Belinda's orbit. She noticed early that in any gathering he withdrew into himself to a point where he presented an appearance of hauteur. When she tackled him about it he said defensively, "All they ever talk about is that magazine. You'd think it was the first book of the Bible."

"Well, it *is* new, and it is their livelihood, mine too, and it is where we spend a third of our waking hours."

"But it isn't your sole topic of conversation," said Norman, triumphant.

It was one thing to get a little nettled at him herself; it was another when criticism came from without. At lunch one steamy August day, Zari Zulalian of the art department said, "You know what Norman reminds me of?"

Her dark eyes grew so dreamy that Belinda prepared herself to hear something pleasant. "That new miracle bonding stuff," said Zari, "that you have to be very careful not to get on your fingers if you don't want to find yourself wearing made-to-order gloves."

"He's new in town—"

"Five months is new?"

"—and you've met him all of what, twice?"

"The Zulalians have second sight," said Zari speedily, and glanced at her watch. "I was going to duck into a bookshop on the way back to the office, but there isn't time." She gave Belinda one of her white and slightly ironic smiles. "Time certainly flies when you're having a difference of opinion."

They didn't know Norman, thought Belinda with conscious loyalty. For some time she had been aware of a growing "they"—even her parents on the occasion when she had driven him down to Bedlington in a burst of gratitude for his having cured her car of stalling at every other red light; it was something to do with the dwell angle.

The Graces were more than civil, providing toasted cheese sandwiches and beer and an attentive audience for Norman's backpacking adventures. Norman knew that they were travel writers, but did not overdo his deference in recounting a Kentucky experience at which they broke into spontaneous laughter. An onlooker would have said that for a first meeting it had gone remarkably well. Belinda brooded grimly all the way back to Boston.

The incident might have been a prelude to what happened in October, when after telephoned debates during the day it was agreed that Jeb Moulton would pick Belinda up as arranged in spite of the approach of a somewhat diminished hurricane; it was the last evening of a much-touted musical headed for New York.

In the lobby, it also turned out to be one of the infrequent evenings when the Bests invited Norman to dinner. When Belinda had performed introductions, he ran an unraveling eye over Jeb from head to foot and gave her a concerned little frown. "Should you be going out with a hurricane coming?"

It wasn't so much the words as a proprietariness that bordered on the husbandly. "Yes," said Belinda, as startled as if she had stepped on something sharp in the dark, "and right away, too, as Jeb has a cab waiting."

Which he would take to be a deliberate cruelty, she thought as the closing elevator doors gave her a last glimpse of his tightly compressed lips; for the moment at least he did not run to taxis. Zari's observation came back with clarity, but on the way to the theater Belinda managed to dismiss it. She had been his first friend in Boston, and without thinking about it he had acquired an overprotectiveness.

And the wind and rain were wild enough; even the driver, pulling up under the marquee, said laconically, "This must be some show."

*37*

It was only that. Norman was not intending to set up shop as her custodian.

Except that he was there in the lobby when they got back, exhilarated by music and lyrics and dazzling tropical scenery that would not be swamped by the storm. Jeb saw him first through the lobby's inner door, a vigilant figure seated on the chair beside the elevator.

"The lights in this dormitory will be out at eleven o'clock sharp," Jeb said lightly to Belinda, kissing her in a graze under the watchful swivel of Norman's head. "I'll call you."

Until tonight he had seen her inside her apartment even if he didn't stay for a liqueur. His taxi cruised away. Belinda let herself into the lobby, walking with erectness over the strip of black rubber matting to Norman, who was plucking from the top of his folded military-surplus raincoat, a long-skirted garment they had both laughed about a great deal, a transistor radio, which he flourished in Exhibit-A fashion. .

"I was worried about you. A man was struck by a flying—"

Like spanking a child, it had to be done in the heat of the moment. Belinda pressed the elevator button and gathered her courage. "If you do this again, Norman," she said, realizing too late that it was a mistake to allow for such a possibility, "I won't be home if you come and I will hang up if you call."

She had never spoken like that to anyone before, but mixed with her anger was an incipient alarm. So as not to see more than a second of his instant pallor she watched the indicator over the closed doors—four, three, two—and Norman said tightly, "Don't say that, Belinda. Don't *say* it. If you really meant it, I'd—"

"Then it's simple," said Belinda, stepping into the finally arrived elevator and forcing herself to smile. "Just don't do it."

She went to bed feeling that she had left something unavoidably, uncomfortably, in tatters.

There was a test sooner than she had expected. Her twenty-sixth birthday, about which she had told nobody for fear of forcing flowers for her desk, or worse, a ceremonial little lunch, coincided with the eve of her parents' departure for Europe. Because her father was nursing a problematical tooth, she met them for dinner at their hotel.

A small box tendered at the outset contained earrings, slender almonds of deep polished jade dropping from lacy gold, which Belinda put on at once with the aid of her propped-open compact. "They're nice with your eyes," said Elizabeth Grace, and there was a little spatter of applause from the next table, where the operation had been watched with an air of deep involvement.

Farewells over a cointreau, and the usual admonitions to voyagers abroad. Mrs. Grace retired upstairs to do something complicated to her hair, and Belinda's father insisted on seeing her home in a taxi, tooth or not. They would be gone for six weeks, photographing and filling journals with notes, which would eventually come together in the form of short pieces and later a book. It was, considered Belinda, a nearly ideal way to make a living.

She would not let her father get out into the cold air—"It can't be a good idea at the eleventh hour"—and called a last thank you and used her key with only the barest trace of apprehension.

Saturday mornings were sacrosanct, by and large, and her telephone did not ring until a considerate eleven-fifteen. Belinda heard Norman's voice with a kind of ashamed relief; whatever the necessity, she had been cutting to him.

And then he said reproachfully, "Why didn't you tell me it was your birth—"

A frozen and appalled silence plunged both ways along the line. In it, inescapably, was a waiting and tireless shape unseen in a doorway close enough to hear words called onto the icy air. Belinda put the receiver back with a finality all the more sure because of its quietness; there was no furious impulse here, no quirkish temper.

For the first time in her sunny and successful life she was

frightened, not passingly, as at the black crouch of a nightmare or when a second X-ray was required in the course of a routine physical, but deep-down frightened, and there was no one in whom she could confide without a compassionate, "I could have told you that."

Zari Zulalian would not say it, but it would be all over her vivid expressive face. There had been an implied warning in Jeb Moulton for all his lightness.

Her fault, her willful blindness as to what was happening to what she had thought was a pleasant, no-strings companionship. But where had Norman Comstock come from in the sense that mattered, out of whose life might he have been sharply expelled?

She stayed in her apartment all that day, not answering her phone when it rang again at noon, at four, at seven. When there was a knock at her door late the next morning, and Norman called, "Belinda, at least let me know you're all right," she called back levelly, "I am perfectly all right."

This was how wives with undislodgeable ex-husbands must feel, except that they could get a court injunction. And Norman had not threatened her; he had if anything threatened himself. Belinda recognized that to be the ultimate in emotional blackmail; on the other hand, people capable of rash dramatics generally spoke of them first.

I am talking about suicide, she thought, staying in all the next day, too, although she was reduced to two strips of bacon, a can of black bean soup for which she had no lemon, an egg she didn't dare eat because it had a crack in it and now was the time salmonella would catch up with her and prove fatal, a slice plus a crust of thin rye bread, a miniature of rum from some forgotten occasion, and approximately two glasses of white wine, which she saved like a miser for the evening.

But not Norman, not a man who treasured his body to the point of gargling. Apart from everything else he was, even if agreeably so, far too self-centered.

Belinda solaced herself uneasily with that, going to bed to

the accompaniment of rain, which presently changed to sleet. When she was waked by an imperative and repeated knocking on her door, she got up with a mixture of expectation and dread, having difficulty with the sleeves of her robe.

"Who is it?"

"Police."

Two of them, uniformed, eyeing her with a professional sympathy and curiosity that telegraphed its message even before they handed her Norman's familiar thin black wallet, rubbed around the edges; she had planned to get him a new one for Christmas.

Although tears kept Belinda from deciphering it at once, Norman had—how many pondering hours after she had hung up on him and then called coldly through her door?—written her the promised poem.

Small wonder that in their brief and awkward presence there, explaining that there had been a number of witnesses to Norman Comstock's throwing himself deliberately under a late train pulling into South Station, the two policemen had stared fascinatedly at her floor.

# Chapter

# Six

The lines in Norman's recklessly bad handwriting had been scrawled on the back of a greeting card torn in half:

*Don't follow me*
*I would not take you from your mirrors and blue rugs*
*To my dark place*
*But will you smile sometimes at my reflected face*
*And set your feet in my blue footsteps there?*

On the other side, he had blacked out a short printed verse and written, "Please deliver to Miss Belinda Grace" and her address.

Dazedly, Belinda signed a form in receipt of the wallet and its itemized contents: twelve dollars, Social Security card, driver's license, watch repair ticket, and "poem?" Blankly, like a child presented with a baffling object, she asked, "What should I do with it?"

She didn't even know what she meant, unless possibly that

it seemed wrong for her to be in possession of anything of Norman's. The older policeman shrugged. "He must have wanted you to have it; a lady saw him throw it down on the platform just before he took his dive."

He tore his gaze from the rugs, the blue footsteps continuing to elude him, and made an inquisitive assessment of the room. "I guess you had a fight?"

From their manner, they believed that Norman had shared the apartment, and Belinda did not bother to correct them. She said simply, "Yes," even though it seemed to fill the air with shouts, accusations, unheeded threats.

She only pretended to listen when they told her which station house could give her further details. The tears had been like a flash flood, over too soon and leaving her with nothing to do but tremble very slightly with the passion of her wish that they would go away and leave her alone to stare at this terrible thing and her part in it.

It showed. They turned precipitately toward the door, the younger one saying cautiously, as if it fell well outside regulations, "If I were you I'd take something, miss. A drink, I mean," he added hastily.

*Don't follow me.* "Thank you. I will."

And she did, when the elevator had commenced its shuddering descent; she made herself a cup of tea and poured the whole magnificent 1.6 ounces of rum into it.

She thought, carefully keeping anything else at bay although this was the solitude she had wanted, that in the morning— no, later in the morning—she would go to the house where Norman had had a room and see if there was an address book. The police knew where his driver's license had been issued, and would presumably pass the information along to their opposite numbers in Pennsylvania, but she ought to call, or send a note.

Saying what? "Your son was trying to take over my life and took his own instead, and I didn't believe him when he hinted that he might?"

Her mind backed away.

It was a temptation, to keep out the cold, to wrap herself in the cheapest kind of comfort. Norman's emotional balance must have been precarious; if it had not been she, it would have been someone else; even brother's keepers did not always know what went on in the brother's head.

But she should not have been influenced even half-consciously by the people who tended to shy away from Norman. She could have opened her door when he knocked, and sat down patiently with him and explained that although she liked him and appreciated his company she had to be free to do whatever she pleased and see whomever she pleased.

She could have urged him toward counseling, available for the asking in any large city. (But how did one do that? "You strike me as getting stranger and stranger, Norman"?)

It had become three o'clock, but the images piled themselves up like a relentless home movie. Norman helping her feed the ducks on the Common. Depressed about a dauntless little girl with a bobbing-up-and-down hole in the heel of her sock: "But if I gave her the money for a new pair I might be hauled in as a child molester, the way things are now."

Late one Sunday morning when they were to drive up to Vermont to look at the leaves, he had stopped to rescue a terrified cat incarcerated in the wire around a sidewalk tree and being barked at by a dog and had been well scratched for his pains. In spite of washing and Merthiolate from Belinda's medicine cabinet, he had peered apprehensively at his wrists for a good part of the journey.

Belinda fell asleep in her chair, head at an uncomfortable angle, because it seemed the final rejection to say in effect, "Too bad, Norman," and return snugly to bed. She was waked by a repeated summoning sound, which resolved itself into knuckles on her door.

Even though she had never slept sitting up in her living room before, she knew at once why she was there, chilled and stiff. She called, "Just a minute," and got up, bending to retrieve a slipper that had fallen off during the night. This was unmistakably authority again, and the horrifying thought crossed her mind, as it should have hours ago, that a man's wallet did not always go with his body.

They might demand, if they could do that, that she come with them and look . . .

From the high banding of cold, new sunlight on the building across the street she guessed the time to be about seven o'clock. She drew back the bolt and, hand on the chain, said her automatic, "Who is it?"

He had a head cold. "Police."

She was fooled to the end. When she opened the door a verifying two inches, Norman stood there, smiling a little anxiously but clearly pleased with himself. After a fleeting examination of what he had wrought during the small hours, he said triumphantly, "There, you see? You *are* in love with me."

Belinda imagined that she could actually feel the blood draining from her face, leaving it a dizzied white; draining from elsewhere too, perhaps to puddle from her knees down, so that she wouldn't be able to move.

But she could and did move the few steps to the bookcase on whose top she had laid Norman's wallet. For purely physical reasons she didn't dare try to speak. She tore the scrawled-on portion of greeting card once down the middle and once across, thrust everything through the door, closed and relocked it, and, hand clamped over her mouth, wove her way to the bathroom.

Because the day before had been one of enforced semifasting, her violent efforts left her with a rasped throat and an updrift of tiny, fiery sparks before her eyes. The sparks could not obliterate the shapes of the "policemen": card-company cohorts, dressed in uniforms rented from a theatrical-supply house?

If Belinda had not been so stunned by the tangible evidence of Norman's wallet, if she had not been half preparing herself for some shocking move, there would undoubtedly have been deviations to be spotted in those uniforms. The badges, for instance—but she hadn't even asked for identification.

In retrospect, and by morning sun instead of lamplight and the disorientation of having been jerked out of sleep, the visit had been far too simple and nonquestioning. Even in a city the size of Boston a suicide could not be dismissed as summarily as a test pancake.

But then, who could gauge her naivete better than Norman?

Still, the cruelty of it, and the terrifying will behind it. Had he really thought that after a night of self-recrimination, which she had indeed indulged in, she would fall into his arms with forgiving joy?

And was he under the mistaken impression, after his visit to the house in Bedlington, that there was a great deal of money in the background, ripening like a peach?

Although she had heard nothing from the hall, Belinda was seized abruptly by wave after wave of chills. In her bedroom, she glanced at the clock and called Zari Zulalian in Pippin. She said with what she believed to be perfect calm that something had happened to make it impossible to stay in her apartment, and could she avail herself of Zari's couch?

"Sure." The tiniest of wondering pauses, but not followed by any question. "Tell you what, I was planning to go into the office a little late anyway so I'll stop by with the key."

She was there in under half an hour, which indicated some wary watching of the rear-view mirror. She gazed narrowly at Belinda and felt her forehead. "You've got flu or something. Why don't you take some aspirin and pack a bag while I make us a cup of coffee?"

The civilized thing to do was demur, but the thought of being incapacitated here—what might Norman do, what tale concoct for the superintendent?—was insupportable, and in any case Zari had already been exposed. Belinda said in a voice made unreliable by gratitude, "Thank you, this is so far above and beyond the call. . . . You were right about Norman.

He had me believing most of the night that he had committed suicide on the tracks in South Station.''

"Oh, that total bastard,'' said Zari with feeling, and let it go at that.

She drove them to Pippin in Belinda's car, leaving behind a street of nine-fifteen Monday-morning emptiness. "I hate people to talk to me when I'm sick. That seat tilts back, doesn't it? You might even sleep.''

It was a virulent, bone-cracking strain of flu. For four days, even lying in Zari's bedroom with its warm honey-colored walls, the small of Belinda's back ached as if a monstrous tooth had been implanted there. Most of the mainly liquid nourishment she forced down did not stay there, and on the fifth morning, when she stripped the bed, put on fresh sheets, and removed herself to the couch, she was damp with effort.

She was also and finally sure, after fragmentary examinations during feverish nights and half-sleeping daylight hours, that she did not want and in fact could not bring herself to pick up her life where she had left it off.

It wasn't only Norman's persistence—Zari had seen him twice across the street from the building that housed the magazine offices—or the fact that for the present at least the apartment in which she had taken such pleasure was thoroughly spoiled. *My blue footsteps*. It was what had happened to her when she opened her door the morning after shock and tears and images: the utter, crashing destruction of her confidence in herself.

When sudden allover damage occurred to the glaze on pottery, it was called crazing. It was, thought Belinda, an apt term.

Everybody else—her parents, Jeb Moulton, Zari, and the other people she knew at the magazine—had seen the possibility of trouble in Norman. If she had been capable of that basic an error in judgment, what other mistakes had she made along the way, what giant blunder would she commit next?

Her job involved frequent decisions, and by their very nature decisions required a conviction of sureness. That had been stripped from her. Just now, faced with a shopping choice between two frozen vegetables, she would have to buy both or neither.

Zari had clearly been thinking along the same lines, with the added reflection that, although this place was too small for a pair of anything except newlyweds, Belinda, noticeably thinner, was in no shape to go out into the weather and hunt for new quarters, either here or in Boston.

She said that evening, "You're going to want some time to get better and sort yourself out. Why don't we just switch for a few weeks?"

It was an idea Belinda had entertained but dared not suggest.

"Your landlord, Mr. Tregovia, looks amenable enough, if you give me a note containing some believable lie," said Zari, "and if I find any of Norman's footprints lying around I'll stamp all over them."

Mr. Tregovia, although in his sixties, had indeed been taken visibly with Zari's dark eyes, black fringe, bold nose, dashing smile.

"But what about here?"

"They wouldn't give a damn, I don't think, as long as you didn't have screaming parties or bring in a zoo," said Zari. "There isn't even a real superintendent. Donald Aintree downstairs serves as that, for half-rent, although nobody dares call on him very often because he's a writer."

Here she paused meditatively. "He wears very daunting-looking glasses, but only in the morning. I think they're made of clear glass. The landlady lives out on the Point and she's half batty anyway. If you said you were me with dyed hair you might well get away with it."

Belinda said, "Norman will come calling on you." Her stomach flickered.

"Good, I hope he does. I'll tell him you were called to New York to the bedside of your former fiancé, a karate blackbelt, and there's a reconciliation on the horizon. That ought to settle his hash," said Zari. "Are you all right for funds?"

Even at auction the Chinese rugs had been an extravagance, and extra large dinners over a period of months added up surprisingly; there were buried but related expenses in that column as well.

"Not to the point of where I wouldn't appreciate a job of some kind," said Belinda.

"You can't even consider it for another few days, but in the meantime," this was meat and drink to Zari, a born arranger of schemes, "I have a whole slew of aunts who know everything and everybody in Pippin. I'll start them on the scent right away."

Which was how Belinda had come to be leaving the animal clinic in the close vicinity of another reported death in the night.

Even on so short an acquaintance, it was hard to think of Deb Kingsley in the past tense. Dedicated to her job, for all her nonchalance about it. At ten minutes before twelve, flushed with cold and breathless from running; at shortly after twelve, her breath stopped forever.

How long was shortly?

The sweeping rain had begun as Belinda left the parking lot; say four or five minutes of twelve. The windshield wipers could not keep up with the first drenching force, and her progress had been slowed although the road was by now a very familiar one. A driver unfamiliar with the territory would have been further hampered.

There had been a watch-repair ticket in Norman's wallet.

But that was almost five weeks ago, Belinda reminded herself steadyingly. The chances were that he had picked up the watch long since and it was keeping accurate time. (But don't forget that the rain might have begun earlier somewhere between Boston and Pippin.)

According to Zari, Norman had not come knocking on the door after all, which was reassuring on the one hand and—in view of his two appearances across the street from the office building—suspect on the other. Still, how could he know where she was, where and what hours she worked?

This was like a child imagining a tiger under the bed—but instantly, in Belinda's mind, the tiger began to brood dangerously over a locked door, scraps of a torn-up poem, a successful vanishing. She jumped to her feet and did what she had undertaken to do five minutes ago: called Zari back.

This extremely late contact between them wasn't unusual. With personal calls firmly discouraged at the clinic and not particularly smiled on at the magazine either below an exalted level, it was the only opportunity to discuss problems that might have arisen in their arrangement at either end.

And mail. Although they forwarded each other's routinely, there was an occasional envelope that looked as if its contents should be communicated at once. Zari had the habits of a night watchman and was still lively at the hour when Belinda's post-midnight repast was in the process of cooking.

At thirty, she had not known the much younger Deb Kingsley but had gone to school with an older sister. Told about the murder, she said, "How frightful," and, soberly and in an echo of millions of voices all over the globe, "The world gets a little scarier every day."

Belinda agreed that it did. For that matter, this apartment had gotten a little scarier in the past two minutes, however illogically. She said, staring at one of Zari's flaring, foaming seascapes, "It may sound paranoid to ask, but still no sign of Norman?"

"Not that I've seen," said Zari troubledly, "but I heard the Bests talking on the stairs tonight, they were coming down while I was going up—"

And, silk-footed in its muscled stripes, the tiger moved.

# Chapter
# Seven

"All right, that's enough," said Cherry Aintree, twitching folds of blue flannel fastidiously away from the eager approach of Roger's nose. "Go and lie down like a good dog."

Hattie could not help a reluctant admiration for Laurence's wife. Unlike the others, whatever they might be feeling when they encountered him in the town, she made no bones about her coolness toward a usurping animal, and one without papers at that.

She had dropped by unexpectedly on this late morning for a reason so far unstated. It was certainly not just to see Hattie, whom she had summed up with detached exactitude on her arrival: soft old skirt that had never been guarded by a taffeta slip, rose cardigan with objects in the pockets, comfortable slippers, gray hair more wayward than usual because of its vigorous washing in the shower earlier.

Cherry had accepted a cup of coffee—"If you're sure it's no bother"—and was graceful with the creamy Belleek cup and saucer. Her own cashmere sweater matched her skirt.

There were tiny pearls in the earlobes just visible inside dark hair so faultlessly smooth that from a short distance it might have been painted on.

Her lipstick, a clear raspberry red, was just as immaculate against her fine pale skin. Hattie reflected that she and Laurence, quite apart from any other sensations, must hold each other in mutual, critical high esteem.

To say, "What can I do for you?" to such a creature was bald, but Hattie said it anyway and Cherry gave a contrived little start. "I was just," she nodded at a corner of the living room, "looking at the desk. I don't know how many conversations Aunt Charlotte and I had about it."

The tone was wistful, remembering, suggestive of promises from Charlotte. What an acquisitive girl she is, thought Hattie, and said with innocence, "It is a nice old piece, isn't it?"

The perfect eyebrows drew tinily. "Actually, I stopped in because Laurence has had a stubborn cough for a week and the usual things don't seem to be helping. He says Aunt Charlotte had a marvelous concoction."

Roger sprang out of his basket, barking, and the door knocker was used with force. Hattie, suspecting who this was, could have wrung her hands.

The man who stood on the step had a totally hairless ivory head and a wispy black Fu Manchu mustache. Hattie glanced past him at the truck marked "Stowell Electric" and whisked herself outside, on the pretext of not letting in anymore cold air, before he had gotten past "You called about—"

"Yes, I have a fence that I want electrified. Could you come back this afternoon, as I have guests?"

The eerie head shook with decision. "Have to be some time next week then."

Hattie was torn. She flinched from the prospect of all those walks with Roger, particularly after dark, and she was well aware—such was the way of Pippin—that if she turned the estimator away for so frivolous a reason he would be in no hurry to return even if business was slow. As opposed to that, even though in her nursing career she had faced situations that would have sent another woman fleeing for the nearest exit, was her fear of the Aintrees' finding out.

Especially Cherry. Not for the first time, Hattie thought that, smartly uniformed, she would make a good, unruffled head for a firing squad.

But, she realized, the hollow corner in the back was invisible from the living room. In fact, unless Cherry moved from her comfortable chair to the fireplace end of the room, she couldn't see the other spot Hattie had in mind either.

She led the fence man quickly around the far end of the house, arms crossed tightly over her cardiganed chest, slippered feet growing icy from the sodden twig-strewn ground. When she had pointed out Roger's run and answered a few questions about outlets and voltage, she said, "If there's anything else, will you call me, please? This is to be a surprise."

The man uttered a little snort of amusement, which Hattie took to be a comment to the effect that there was always an element of surprise in an electric fence, and whipped out a steel tape measure. She let herself in at the back and stood shivering over the floor register in the living room while she gave the excuse that had popped into her head.

"Sorry, that was an electrician." As if Cherry would not have done some instant craning at the truck. "The outside light blew halfway down last night, and I'm afraid of dangling wires."

"Oh, I'm sure Donald could have fixed that for you. He's moved out to the old Steptoe house on Currant Road and pays reduced rent for doing repairs." There was a pleased, curled-lip quality to Cherry's voice. "Laurence had me go over there the other day to get his signature on something and he was called away to unstop a sink. At least he said it was a sink."

Why the beautifully groomed, pearl-earringed spite? Hattie's wonder lasted only for seconds. Laurence's wife undoubtedly considered herself safe with this old-fashioned, unworldly family relative in slippers, but what had not been bred in the Irish

*53*

bone had been taught in recovery rooms, at bedsides, by the lips of unstrung survivors.

"Laurence had me go over there" could be translated as "I volunteered." But Cherry must have been exposed to Donald's occasional girls. How had she thought she could compete, even if Laurence didn't exist?

Hattie said, "In a house this old I feel safer with a professional," and added as Cherry stood up with another of her Roger-induced sneezes, "Charlotte's cough remedy was really nothing more than honey and lemon with a dash of apricot brandy."

"Oh." Cherry, losing interest, checked abruptly in the buttoning of her coppery suede coat. Hattie turned.

Whitey had come strolling into the room. He paused at the sight of Cherry, who was new to him, dismissed her with the flick of an erect tail end, seemed to contemplate a frontal assault on Roger's basket, and sauntered down the rug instead.

"You don't let him on the settee, of course," said Cherry with cool authority.

Hattie did not, as it happened. Charlotte had treasured that particular piece of furniture, and it would have been an insult to allow the old bottle-green velvet to be clawed casually to shreds. She had taught the cat very quickly by employing a plant mister.

But Cherry's deference over whether a cup of coffee would be any trouble had departed. She was back to basics: the bringing-to-heel of a dowdy incompetent.

"Only in the evenings," said Hattie.

Who? wondered Donald Aintree.

The choice wasn't large. There was a bare possibility of one of the other tenants, inquisitive about the sound of his typewriter; occasionally, if he was only making a brief trip to the cellar, he left his door slightly ajar. Phineas Coe, who shared the ground floor, had very prying eyes to go with his little wreath of gray hair—and he had read Donald's book, which he might view as entitling him to enter and take what he would call a tiny peep.

But Donald did not think it had been Phineas Coe.

Cherry? She had stayed long enough on her visit to necessitate the offer of a drink, and the mechanics of that would have given her time. As a rule, she had the noncuriosity of the perfectly self-satisfied, but the matter under consideration involved research rather than the indulging of idle interest.

Peter Farris, on the other hand, was curious about everything: the apple crop in Washington, how much other people's dentists charged for root canals, how to make Lancashire shepherd's pie. His very light eyes raced impatiently ahead of what he was being told, so that unwary interlocutors often found themselves speaking at a desperate, tongue-trapping speed.

It was Nan who had found out about the vacancy in the old Steptoe house, and as a gesture of appreciation Donald had had them both to dinner shortly after he was settled. At some point during the kitchen preparations one of them, he could not now remember which, had said something to the other about getting cigarettes from the car. There was a slot of time there for a quick, informed dive into the row of small spiral-bound notebooks in the bookcase beside the typewriter.

Everybody in the family knew about them. They weren't diaries, although the weather was sometimes there and Donald entered any events of note, nor could they be called working journals, as apart from a few short stories he had left his typewriter largely alone for two years. They did contain scraps of ideas and bits of physical description: faces and attitudes that struck him as indelible when he saw them but would, he knew, vanish if not committed to paper.

On the back page of each notebook were the kinds of highly usable names, gleaned from the newspapers, mailboxes, television credits, for lack of which a writer might be unreasonably stopped in his tracks for minutes at a time.

On the cover of every one, handily, were the dates spanned within. And some hurried hand, not Donald's, had placed

"February-April" of the preceding year at the very end of the row.

Now, at after three-thirty, someone was coming down the stairs in a quick, light way impossible for Mrs. Calvacaressi. Belinda Grace, who was temporarily occupying the Zulalian girl's apartment. Donald had memorized her face, but for obscure reasons of his own had not penciled a single word of description.

It was Saturday. He pulled wider the door, which, after his working hours of roughly nine-thirty to twelve, he left a crack open so as to oblige the fellow tenants whom he had more or less bullied into not disturbing him in the mornings. There wasn't, in this old house, a buzzer system.

He said lightly, "I heard the constabulary last night. Is everything all right?"

". . . Well, no." The haunted look she had had upon Donald's first introduction to her was back, in a trace of lilac under her clear, arched eyes. "An attendant at the animal clinic was killed a few minutes after I left. She was only nineteen."

Donald frowned at her in sympathy. "Drugs again?"

"No, whoever it was—" The quick head-shake that accompanied was stilled as if a muscle had suddenly refused its function. The gaze that she had simply forgotten to take away from his was inward, blind, and, peculiar in this context, hopeful. Without another word, she let herself out of the house.

In his apartment again, door firmly closed to aid concentration, Donald considered his next move. He had already made one fruitless telephone call. To put his particular question to Cherry would have roughly the same effect as asking a member of the women's sodality whether she had been at the poor box lately, and there was a cogent reason for not asking Nan.

Wait; Laurence and Cherry had celebrated their ninth wedding anniversary in February and, untypically, made a family gathering out of it; younger members only, as Charlotte Ivy no longer went out in the evening. Cherry might have decided to seek out his private opinion of the dinner at their country club; intrusive of her but no more than that.

And here it was: "Feb. 19. Roads finally clear. L. and C.'s 9th so all hands present at the P.C.C. Drawling girl for me, Mayflower type, but all festive with oysters, roast beef, wine."

No harm there. Donald closed the notebook and put it back where it belonged. He had almost convinced himself that he had nothing to worry about.

Apart from establishing the fact of virginity, by no means standard at her age, the autopsy report on Deborah Kingsley had no surprises for the police. A .22 bullet that had lodged against a rib was turned over, to join the one that had exited, but in a seacoast town the chances of finding the weapon itself were so small as to be negligible.

When Hallam returned to the Kingsley house in mid-afternoon as arranged, her parents had managed to fill in their younger daughter's last week on earth. On the surface at least it wasn't the stuff of which murder was made. College classes in Boston four days a week, by dint of which, along with summer sessions, Deborah was determined to get her degree and go on to veterinary training.

It wasn't easy to get into those schools. Her grade-point average of 3.9 would have helped, but with the tremendous number of applicants experience had the real edge; hence the job at the clinic. Between that and the long hours of studying, her social life had been minimal.

Boyfriends? A Harvard junior with whom she had managed an occasional weekend date. Before that? Mrs. Kingsley saw the trend of that at once. "None of those terrible emotional breakups, if that's what you mean. Deb was so single-minded about . . ."

Her eyes filled with tears. "Are you fond of animals, Lieutenant?"

Into Hallam's memory, unwelcomely, flashed the coatimundi

that Sue had brought home from a wild-animal farm for no better reason than that they had sold their last descented skunk. For a whole unforgettable month it had sat in its cage in their living room, spitting out fruit peels and seeds to join the litter of shredded newspaper poked through the bars. Hallam thought he could scarcely wait for the hot weather, when there would be flies. Across the room from it, more often than not, the fox terrier that Sue had adopted barked at regular, head-splitting intervals.

Of the coatimundi, Sue had said reproachfully, "You haven't even tried to tame it," and Hallam, still in thrall and obedient, had donned gloves and attached the light metal leash that had come with the animal. He ought to have been warned by the very length of the leash. Instantly, using its sharp and hideous claws, the coatimundi came streaking up toward his hand.

He said in a tone that would have deceived nobody undistracted by grief, "Yes, I am," thinking with some bitterness that, with idols toppling right and left, a blanket fondness for animals remained sacrosanct.

"Then you'll understand. The idea of being a vet was Deb's life."

The unbearable echo of those words drove Mrs. Kingsley precipitately from the room, her husband following. Hallam waited for a minute or two and then let himself quietly out.

Unconsciously influenced by his own experience, he began to entertain the concept of Deborah Kingsley's being killed because of what she was rather than who she was, as an act of rage and revenge by some half-demented client.

Suppose the equivalent of "little Jade Boy" had not come out of the anaesthetic, and the owner blamed the clinic and staff for negligence? Compared to some of the motives Hallam had unearthed during his years in Homicide, it made eminent sense. And Sergeant Uffi had said there was a dead dog in the freezer.

At the clinic half an hour later, the idea gained strength. It was to shape the entire case.

# Chapter
# Eight

"... about fifty or fifty-five," said Belinda, "and quite red-faced and angry even when he first came in. I got the impression that that was the way he went everywhere."

"Like Mr. MacGregor," suggested Hallam startlingly, and Belinda concealed a faint surprise. "Exactly," she said.

They were in the lounge with its yellow and orange chairs, dieffenbachia contributed by Hilda and suffering from a strange, sallow blight, table with magazines, coffeemaker. Although the clinic was busy as always on weekends—it would remain open continuously until eight o'clock on Monday morning, when its tenants would be collected and returned to their own vets—Dr. O'Neill had not been left unattended. The director had arrived.

There was something godlike about Dr. Kitsch, and it was not only his massively framed six feet plus. He progressed rather than strode, radiating a serene authority as visible as reflected light on his healthily tanned and mostly bald head. Although he was frequently to be found in his office, when he actually took his turn at duty it was as if the board chairman of a large oil company had showed up to man a gasoline pump.

It was his usual weekend practice to hold himself available by beeper. But Deborah Kingsley's murder, still largely unknown in the town because the *Pippin News* was a weekly, would certainly have been chronicled for a Boston evening newspaper by its local correspondent, and he was here to deal with whatever repercussions there might be for the clinic.

Belinda had already told Hallam in outline about the man she had suddenly remembered stamping out with his dog. Unless his name surfaced from the deep it was gone forever; she had torn up the card on which she had written it, not getting as far as adding his address because he had begun raising objections about the release form, and the wastebaskets had been emptied by the early-morning cleaning crew.

Nor had she made any attempt at introducing him to Dr. Cooper, whom she had been driven to call upon for help. In her wrath at his rudeness she had simply said, "Doctor, this man will not sign the release form as it stands."

Hallam took a second look at the printed sheet in his hand. "Why?"

"Because of the line that says the veterinarian reserves the right to treat animals on a priority basis. He crossed that out and wrote in a qualified version."

Hallam waited for further enlightenment, and Belinda obliged.

"If a dog is being stitched up after a bad cut, and another is brought in in shock, the final stitches can wait but the shock can't. Dr. Cooper explained that, but the man obviously thought that in being willing to pay for X-rays—he said the dog was vomiting blood—he was buying the entire clinic for the duration."

"And he left in an ugly mood?"

"By understatement. He called us a number of names, one of which doesn't strictly apply to women, and said we'd better hope his dog—a shepherd cross, twelve," said Belinda meticulously, as if it mattered, "didn't, his words, die on him. Then he gave the leash a dreadful yank and marched out."

"What time was this again?"

"About ten-thirty. I suppose I was a little unstrung," said Belinda, defensive about not remembering the man's name in the face of Hallam's obvious interest, "because we'd just lost a dog between reception and the examining room. I was carrying it, in fact. We generally ask clients to put their animals on the table, but the woman who had hit it looked on the point of fainting."

"Would that have been the dog in the freezer?" inquired Hallam, and, curiously, when Belinda said yes, "Do you mind any of this?"

His tone managed to enclose the question in brackets, as ungermane, as suddenly personal as, "Do you like artichokes?"

Belinda felt herself color under the judging probe. "Yes, I do, quite often. It's a pity all animals can't be circumstanced like the one in that masterwork," the coolness of her voice and her glance forced Hallam to turn his head and gaze up at the framed print of a ribboned Dalmation puppy in an upturned fireman's helmet, "but at least the ones here are given every chance instead of starving to death or dying by the roadside."

And you can stay after school and write two hundred lines on the blackboard, too, she added silently—and from the front, appreciated for once, there was a wild explosion of barking. "Excuse me."

Two apricot miniature poodles were leaping and shrieking on the ends of their leashes with the apparent intention of getting at and tearing to pieces a giant black husky. A toweled cat on its owner's lap tried frenziedly to escape from the terry folds. The husky was surveying all with calm.

At Belinda's politic "I was afraid for a minute—" the poodle owner, a blond woman in a safety-pinned scarlet cloak, rose to her feet. She said resignedly, "I knew my husband should have brought them. I'll take them outside for a few minutes."

It wasn't a thing that happened often—the most belligerent breeds were apt to turn meek in these surroundings—but the brief interlude had, for Belinda, reversed a decision arrived at reluctantly during the night.

It had also imparted a certain formality to Hallam. On his feet, although Belinda hadn't been gone for more than a minute, he said, "You didn't connect the telephone call from Warner with the man who had taken his dog away in a temper over an hour earlier. Could it have been the same voice, keeping in mind that he was using a civil tongue the second time?"

Belinda supposed so.

"Any impression as to whether the call might have come from a booth?"

Because, granted a deadly intent, he either lived alone or would have gone out to make arrangements; that was not an appointment he would want overheard. Belinda thought, and shook her head.

Hallam picked up the coat he had dropped over the back of a chair. "As to the dog man's name, you might try thinking about any clear ethnic origin, or whether it was short or took up a fair amount of space on the card. Or what he was wearing. You never know what will jar something loose. . . . What was the dog's name?"

Belinda took this as another appraising little jab. "Tex," she said remotely.

Hallam seemed to congratulate himself with the tiniest of nods, and paused in the doorway to ask what cleaning service the clinic used.

"I have no idea. The receptionist could tell you."

Do *not*, at least not yet and solely on the basis of what Zari had told her, unroll the saga of Norman for the measuring inspection of Lieutenant Charles Hallam. He would consider her on the one hand a credulous fool not to see where matters were tending; on the other, so besotted with herself as to think

*62*

untiring pursuit by a man she had dismissed the most natural thing in the world.

Belinda was acquainted with homicide investigation only through fiction, but it stood to reason that the dog had been seen by a vet during the past year, if only for the essential parvo shots. Although tomorrow was Sunday Dr. Kitsch would have no difficulty, under the circumstances, in persuading the corporate doctors to open their offices for a methodical check of the active files.

A man planning revenge for days would think of that. A man in a blinding rage might not. Belinda, leaving the lounge, began to tease away at the layers that covered his name.

When she brought the enraged cat back to its owner, its fur clipped for the cleaning out of an infected bite and a shot of antibiotic administered, it was clear that the evening paper had made the rounds of the waiting room.

For the moment there was only an intense curiosity, although a voice saying hushedly, ". . . was talking to Hester Kingsley in the Safeway just last week" broke off at Belinda's approach. Was it because in all likelihood none of these people had had occasion to meet Deb in her three weeks on the graveyard shift? Or did the obedient waiting in chairs along the walls, the shiningly buffed tile, the fact of silent, purposeful activity elsewhere add up to something of a hospital atmosphere?

But when Belinda had lifted the top one of three cards left on the counter by the receptionist and said accordingly, "Mr. Connell?" to a gray-whiskered man with a small mop of a dog on his knees, a woman with a Weimaraner spoke up with briskness.

"Miss? I'm Mrs. Jackman. Will you tell Dr. Kitsch that unless my dog can be seen before it's full dark I'll have to go home?"

And there it was, the first little threat. This is not a safe place to be after nightfall.

"See what you done to yourselves?" asked the old man with sudden glee, dividing a glance between the woman and a long-legged girl in jeans. "Time was, I'd have let you ladies go ahead of me—"

"Maybe at the gate to the cemetery, Joe Connell."

"—but now, you stand aside to let a lady out of an elevator and chances are she'll belt you with her handbag."

He cackled hopefully at Belinda, who only smiled, conducted him into the examining room, signaled Dr. O'Neill on the intercom, and, receiving no answer to her knock on Dr. Kitsch's door, put her head back into reception to tell Mrs. Jackman that she was next and it shouldn't be long.

It wasn't. The tiny dog's trouble, noneating and abdominal discomfort, proved with dramatic swiftness to be the result of gorging. "Mr. Connell," said Dr. O'Neill severely as Belinda began to clean up, "I've warned you that a dog of Wendy's size and age simply cannot tolerate large amounts of rich— No!"

He snatched up the patient, who after the manner of her kind was showing signs of regretting her hasty decision, and thrust her at her owner. "Just water tonight, and a little dry food if she insists."

Night. Threatening to close in with the departure of Dr. O'Neill and the director, looking as magnificent and wrinkle-free as if he had not been napping on his office couch, and the arrival of Dr. Jane Hilary.

X-rays showed that the Weimaraner with the swollen cheek had an ulcerated tooth. Belinda had to be firm about barring Mrs. Jackman from the surgery. A whole world of potential trouble lay in allowing clients to be present at any operation, beginning with objections about having their pet's muzzles tied with round-edged white nylon shoelace before anaesthesia or, in the case of muzzleless dogs, faces covered with a towel.

Surely it wasn't necessary to frighten the poor thing that way? Pandora or Robin or Leo wouldn't hurt a day-old chick— but it wasn't a chick advancing on a dog in the grip of extreme alarm and usually pain; it was a white-coated stranger holding something sharp and shiny.

Tooth extracted, stitches put in with a little drain set in place; Belinda carried the Weimaraner to the cage she had readied and then cleaned up the surgery while Dr. Hilary proceeded to the front with a report and follow-up instructions for the morning. When she came back she said, "That seems to be it for the moment, although there's a card on the counter about shots for a Siamese."

As a rule, shots were not all that urgent unless certification were needed for crossing into another state, and perhaps the girl in jeans had simply grown tired of waiting. Still, Belinda repeated Mrs. Jackman's remark about the coming of darkness, and got a resigned nod.

"I suppose we'll see a little of that for a night or two. If I were the director, I'd have hired the security guard from five-thirty to three-thirty instead of ten to six."

These were bold words, thought Belinda, not unlike criticizing the resting on the seventh day—but then, with even greater flair, Dr. Hilary, who was working on another degree in some undisclosed field, took herself off to Dr. Kitsch's sanctum for the deployment of textbooks, notebooks, index cards.

Fresh needles for the surgery, a time-check on all the inhabitants, and, as requested, a trial run through sample names. Start with Duffy, DiAngelo, Garcia, Schmidt . . .

It was worse than useless; to Belinda it was like having combinations of digits poured into her ear while she was looking for a pencil to write down the telephone number that mattered.

Hallam clearly considered it important, which would seem to indicate that Deb Kingsley's personal life had contained no likely killer. It was true that he was unaware of the existence of Norman Comstock and the monstrous and punishing ego thriving behind that candid face, and of the fact that until she had had it cut short in a semisymbolic gesture Belinda's hair had been the almost-shoulder length of Deb's.

But he did know about the overlapping shifts, and he had

not inquired if Belinda knew of anyone who might want to harm her. As reasoning, it was put on a par with keeping symptoms from a doctor on the theory that if he didn't find anything wrong nothing wrong existed; but for the moment Belinda was going to cling to it and avoid the exposure and the reliving.

What would she have to say anyway? That Zari, readdressing mail for her in the apartment house lobby, had inadvertently dropped an envelope that had been scrupulously returned to the small table by another tenant. That the Bests had been overheard to say to each other, "Wasn't it odd about Norman," observed on the street a couple of days earlier, "not coming up to say hello?"

After her first horrified notion of being padded after and hunted down, Belinda could not believe it either. Men like Norman ground their teeth and went on to greener fields.

How extraordinarily silent the clinic was in its intermittent lulls. Dinner, it could be assumed, and a testy putting off of a drive in the cold and dark: "Half an hour isn't going to make that much difference."

Belinda herself was contributing to the hush, tiptoeing to the laundry room with soiled towels and wincing at the gush of water into the washing machine out of deference to the concentration that emanated from Dr. Hilary at her studies. What field could the master's degree she pursued be in? But if asked, she might reply, and at length.

From nowhere, reassuringly, came the reminder that the clinic would look quite tenanted to a passing eye, spotlit as it was in darkness. Dr. Kitsch had had his wife collect him, so that his Mercedes was there for all to see, and so was Belinda's Ford and Dr. Hilary's Datsun, heretofore parked at the rear. A minimum of three alerted people in here, said the cars to the night; not just two women and a collection of ailing animals.

In another departure from custom, although it was academic

because Deb had let her killer in, the front door was locked. They could not be surprised at any rate.

The telephone rang. Belinda picked it up in the drug room, and heard a sweet voice familiar at once.

"I'm so sorry to bother you," oh, the portent of people in habitual and preliminary apology, "but Jade Boy isn't himself at all."

Just as there were extensions, so were there pads and ballpoint pens. Belinda, preparing to write, asked the questions she had learned: "Had he taken water and some nourishment? Were his functions normal?"

"Yes, but he's so *depressed*. He won't have a thing to do with the dear little squeaky duck I bought him, he simply turns his head away."

Why should it occur to Belinda to be grateful that Hallam was not hearing this? It did not take a great deal of experience in a veterinary clinic to know the proper response, and she said, "That's not an unusual reaction after surgery, Mrs. Windom, especially in the smaller and more sensitive breeds." The right note struck; she could tell it at once. "If he isn't more cheerful by tomorrow, you could give us another call."

When she had hung up, the telephone came to life again under her hand.

She answered. She listened for a second and a half before she put the receiver back, so tremblingly that she missed the cradle.

# Chapter
# Nine

"Something wrong?" asked Dr. Hilary from the doorway. For all her dedication to her books she looked a trifle piqued at the fact that two successive calls had dropped into limbo.

"No. I mean yes," said Belinda, suddenly discarding the unwritten rule that personal matters should be left at home along with exciting reds and surgical greens. She brushed her hair back with a hand that was still unsteady. "A man I—"

"Hold on," said Dr. Hilary brusquely. "Go and sit down in the lounge and I'll be right back."

*Hello, Belinda dear.*

Gentle affection, that might be deemed, unless you had costly knowledge of Norman and knew that he had never used that locution before. Not gentle but pleasurably clamped down; not affection but a deep and leisurely spite.

"Say when," said Dr. Hilary dryly, bringing with her a stir of cold air and decanting the contents of a very small bottle into one of the mugs on the shelf below the coffeemaker. "I always carry an emergency ration in my glove compartment. If you were a dog I'd give you steroids. Now, this man?"

My mirrors and blue rugs and miniatures, thought Belinda with a touch of wildness. The present miniature wasn't rum but brandy. She swallowed half of it, the burn having an accented authority in these unlikely surroundings, and then, because of the older woman's neutral calm, she told her in outline about Norman.

"He's clever," said Dr. Hilary when she had finished. "Calling you 'dear' doesn't constitute a threat; he could have been overheard by a whole roomful of people in perfect safety. He sounds like a type who would have been satisfied if you had let him have the last word at the end of the affair."

"It wasn't an affair in the accepted sense. To think," said Belinda, looking back in wonder, "that he seemed too—familiar for that."

"Even so, he must have a feminine streak," said Dr. Hilary, managing to deliver the opinion without disloyalty. "Well, now that he knows where you are, what— I'll get it."

She caught the telephone in the middle of its second ring. Not troubling with preliminaries, she said a crisp hello and then repeated it before replacing the receiver. "People who dial wrong numbers should have the manners to say so," she said with an annoyance that did not deceive Belinda. "What exactly is it you're afraid Norman will do now?"

A second call; he had not liked being hung up on and assumed that, watched, she could not ignore the ringing.

"I don't know." The straight liquor had already begun to do a little merciful work, enabling Belinda to look at her situation from a microscopic remove. "I don't even know what he may have done already."

"Deb Kingsley, you mean? Oh, I shouldn't think so," said Dr. Hilary with a dispassionate shake of her pony-tailed head. "Even supposing the window glass was blurred, and he was so sure he'd seen you that the gun more or less went off by itself, the last thing he'd do would be draw attention to himself by calling here.''

Unless, of course, his mind was working exactly that way. It was difficult to follow the thought processes of a Norman Comstock, to guess at how much havoc he might be prepared to wreak or how deeply he had managed to cover his tracks.

His spoor, thought Belinda, controlling a shiver, and was glad to have the feral echo of that drowned by the door buzzer. "I'll go," she said to the inquiring lift of Dr. Hilary's eyebrows, so steep that they went out of sight under her gray-threaded auburn bangs, because even if he had called from a phone booth only a few blocks away this would be too elementary for Norman. There would be no sport in it.

She was right. A magnificent black and silver German shepherd was ushered in with a mouthful of embedded porcupine quills, and after its little period of shattered quiet the clinic was back at work again.

A part-Angora cat followed with what proved to be hair balls, and then a puppy biting dementedly at itself with severe eczema, and a strange and goatish white dog for euthanizing, the official term, because it could not be broken of its belief that every quadruped of attackable size was a female in heat.

Belinda did not find the process as distressing as she had feared. Here at least, it was the humane step or the necessary alternative to complex surgery, which the family could not afford if they were to eat that month. In either case, and in the absence of tears or tension, the animals had no reason to dread this final needle any more than the vaccinations undergone all their lives.

Tonight, in addition, there was a layer of what amounted to foam rubber between Belinda and the tasks that had become routine. The only thing that cut through it with real sharpness was the periodic summons of the telephone. She braced herself every time before she answered, but Norman did not say again,

"Hello, Belinda dear." He was letting the implications of that sink in.

That in order to know where she worked he had had to follow her from the house in a borrowed or rented car. That that telephone, too, could come under assault any time he chose. That it needn't even be a matter of the telephone—but he would enjoy that disembodied power, for a time, and Belinda was sure he would call.

Until she could think what to do she would arrange a signal with Zari; but she would talk to Norman once, to say, "I've told the police about you," because now there was no longer a choice.

Voice communication, however brief and whatever the message, broke down a barrier; it was an acknowledgment of sorts, and the thought of it produced a qualm of nausea. That set the stage for what happened at nine-thirty, half an hour before the guard could be expected, and gave her the measure of her own vulnerability.

The buzzer meant a walk-in, as two callers could not have arrived yet. Belinda opened the door to a pair, boy and girl upon close inspection, who might have stepped out of a time capsule. Both had long no-colored hair, both wore shapeless jackets and frayed jeans split to accommodate boots.

They were unaccompanied, and they were warily, alertly sizing up their surroundings.

"Is there something I can do for you?" Belinda asked it briskly and pleasantly over a little stir of fear. At the same time she took a casual step backward in the direction of the counter and telephone, because there was something odd here, something Normanish.

The boy jerked his head toward a door. "Can she use the rest room?"

There were gas stations not more than a mile away in both directions. "Yes, certainly," said Belinda. The trip would take them past the director's office and she could alert Dr.

Hilary to the presence of the boy, who could not very well follow.

But when she half turned in invitation they stayed rootedly still, making a decision with their eyes. At some invisible order from the boy, the girl lifted a bony hand to the zipper of her jacket and began to pull on the tab.

The stir inside Belinda's rib cage became a thrash. They looked down on their luck; they might do anything—and who knew what had really happened to Deb? She managed the three additional steps to the telephone, not taking her eyes off the girl, and found herself looking at a rabbit, brown-touched white, nestled against a shirt that appeared to be made of an old bedspread.

"We barely touched him on the road," said the boy, "and we thought—well, this *is* an emergency clinic."

Was anybody that naive? Not really; the plan had been to decant the rabbit in some corner and flee, but they had lost their nerve. Belinda was so weak-kneed with relief that she didn't think of a card or a form, didn't even ask if they would be responsible.

"I don't know whether we treat wild animals, but bring it along in here."

They followed her into the examining room. Belinda left them there and proceeded on to explain the situation to Dr. Hilary. "They seem to be kids with consciences, but I didn't promise anything."

"Fortunately," said Dr. Hilary, succinct, but at the steel table she made her own assessment of the refugees from the sixties and then turned her attention to the crouched and staring rabbit. She touched it as little as possible, shone a light in its eyes, and administered steroids for shock.

"They don't take well to handling," she said to the sponsors, scrubbing at the sink, "but you could put it in a cardboard box, keep it warm, offer it greens and hope for the best."

When they had gone, she said sternly to Belinda, "Did you

log that rabbit in?'' and Belinda, understanding perfectly, said ''What rabbit?''

. . . But the pervasiveness of Norman, reducing her to real fear in a confrontation with innocent adolescents. Dr. Hilary, taking a close and personal look at her for the second time that evening, said, ''If you're going to go on working here, hadn't you better call the police while there's no one out front and tell them about your man?''

*If.* Not a threat; a practical reminder that when a clinic employee reached this state of nerves it was time, on the grounds of efficiency, for something to be done about it.

From an abstract point of view, the job wasn't one to turn handsprings about; even apart from the dead-end aspect, there was responsibility without the salary to go with it. But Belinda was not in the abstract, and at present losing it—familiar, unexacting except physically—would be like taking off the comfortable coat that had been keeping out the cold. She wasn't ready.

She used the telephone in the main clinic. Lieutenant Hallam wasn't available; would she speak to someone else? It was in connection with the Kingsley case? She could try him at home. The number . . .

It didn't answer. Belinda went on her patrol, got dry bedding for the spaniel who had tipped over his water bowl in the process of coming to, was summoned to the door. Somewhere in the middle of all this, she realized that ever since Norman's call the man she had been instructed to think about, who might not have cared what target his gun found here, had dropped completely out of her mind.

''Hattie.'' Nan Farris paused, taking note of the breathlessness at the other end of the line. ''I'm sorry, I caught you in the middle of something.''

At ten o'clock, Hattie could scarcely explain that she had been outside with Roger, staying close to the house because of the eighteen-degree cold, when she heard the ringing.

"Just cleaning out the pots and pans cupboard," she said, of an undertaking of the week before. "Whitey caught a mouse in the kitchen, so I couldn't put it off any longer."

"You ought to have that marvelous woman of Aunt Charlotte's once in a while," said Nan, but her tone betrayed a faint satisfaction at the vision of the Aintrees' supplanter on her knees in a noisy welter of cooking vessels and discarded newspaper. "Peter and I wondered if you could come to dinner tomorrow night? Nothing elaborate, just family. It's so long since we've all seen you to talk to beyond hello how are you."

Hattie, who had last been in the Farris house nearly a year ago on some forgotten mission for Charlotte, was thoroughly taken aback. She wished the Aintrees well, and was mildly pleased when she encountered any one of them in the town for a quick and casual exchange, but when the three of them were together, looking to her eyes like an advertisement for something expensive, and Peter and Cherry were thrown in, it was the difference between a lamp and a barrage of brilliant lights.

Just to begin with, what would she wear?

She said, temporizing, "Thank you, Nan, but I don't think—"

"I know it's short notice, and in fact it's late right now, but Peter wasn't sure until a few minutes ago that he wouldn't be stuck with a client. If it's the night driving, and I don't blame you, I loathe it, Laurence and Cherry could pick you up," said Nan persuasively. "It's on their way."

Hattie's profession had inured her to night driving in all weathers, and the fact of her own car would leave her a free agent. She told Nan the first part of that, added that she would like very much to come, and lowered the mouthpiece to say severely to Roger, who, revitalized by the cold, was scratching at the mattress of his basket as if on his way to China, "Stop that, sir!"

The "sir" came even more naturally to her than his name;

74

it was the form of rebuke she had always used to her male cats and sometimes, forgetfully, her females.

"Cleaning out the pots and pans cupboard indeed," said Nan, laughing. "Is six o'clock all right for you? Good, we'll look forward."

After her admonishment to him Hattie had kept her eye fixed sternly on Roger, who had sat down in his basket to await further developments but, for such a biddable dog, was staring back with a trace of insubordination. When she had hung up, she crossed to his corner and tipped him briskly out.

Like all towns, Pippin had an occasional dog poisoning, sometimes out of feuding malice but generally attributable to raids on chicken yards. There was no way of knowing how Roger felt about chickens in their live and nimble state, but he had been gone for an unguessable period of time the day before and, if he had brought back some dangerous object from his travels, could have retrieved it on one of his after-dark walks, if it were small, without Hattie's noticing.

But when she picked up the mattress he had been scraping at, there was nothing under it but one of his chew sticks, unattractively covered with lint, and half of a rubber frog; once they had lost their squeak he was ruthless with his toys.

I told you so, said Roger behind his whiskers, but he had resented this invasion of his private quarters and trotted challengingly along with Hattie when she went to the back door and tossed the stick and rubber legs into the trash can.

The reason behind Cherry's visit and Nan's dinner invitation wasn't far to seek, and Hattie faced it sturdily. The trust would revert to the estate and be dissolved upon Roger's demise, but the house and everything in it was hers outright.

She could leave everything, including the antiques and the handsome Ivy silver, to a friend or penniless ex-patient if she chose. After a decorous waiting period, she was being reminded where her loyalties lay.

Ten years ago, Hattie had made her will with the lightheartedness of someone whose assets were negligible: her small house to Donald, the few Aintree heirlooms that had found their way into her branch of the family to be divided between Laurence and Nan.

That was changed now. Better make an appointment with Bernard Odom, reflected Hattie, writing herself a note to do so and fortunately forgetting that Charlotte had come to the same decision shortly before her death. And, in the meantime, pray that no moths or crickets had gotten into the muted-green knit suit that was her closest approach to a dinner garment.

The suit was safe except for an odd bleached spot on the front of the jacket; but her train of thought was not so easily broken. The Callahans were not particularly long-lived; both Hattie's parents had died at seventy. As a rule of thumb, that gave her eight more years—but the dog who was responsible for her having to make a new will wasn't yet two. Surely, protected from traffic and checked by a vet at regular intervals, he could be expected to live past the age of ten.

How peculiar. Hattie would have to provide for Roger's future, too.

# Chapter
# Ten

The tan-uniformed security guard was a large, rosy man upon whom his holstered revolver looked as natural as his tie. Belinda was delighted to see him. For one thing, his vigilant presence in a chair opposite the door meant that they could revert to the usual practice of leaving it unlocked until midnight, so that she did not have to drop whatever she was doing quite as quickly at the sound of the buzzer.

It was just as well. Hard on the guard's heels came a Labrador in evident distress. X-rays showed a torsion, a dramatic twisting of the stomach that usually resulted from violent exercise on top of a large meal. The air stoppage effected a breeding ground for bacteria, which throve in airlessness, and, unless the condition was speedily corrected, death.

When the suturing was almost completed, the spaniel owner arrived, wrote a check with a curiously complacent air, and, when Belinda carried the dog out to him, delved into a pocket for a large chunk of ham, extricated from waxed paper, which he popped triumphantly into the spaniel's mouth. He then crumpled the paper, lobbed it into a corner, nodded victoriously at Belinda and departed.

The guard, who was teaching himself Spanish with the aid of a grammar and a workbook, looked on in amazement. "What was that about?"

"I have no idea," said Belinda, retrieving the ball of paper.

Jade Boy's owner did not call again, but there were two masculine inquiries about symptoms in animals treated on the early shift. Belinda, conscientious about analyzing before she transferred them to Dr. Hilary, did not recognize either voice.

In an interlude of quiet she went out to the reception area for the Boston evening newspaper, which had been obligingly tucked into the magazine rack. While the guard murmured, "Estuve, estuviste, estuvo," with the air of a man at his devotions, she took the paper over to the counter and spread it out.

Page five carried an outside shot of the building over the headline: "GIRL, 19, SHOOTING VICTIM AT TROUBLED NORTH SHORE CLINIC." Even though neither position nor salary warranted blind allegiance on Belinda's part, that seemed a little unfair, as if the tragedy was the latest in a long chain of sinister events.

Because of the paucity of detail—two shots fired at close range, no witnesses and no motive established for the killing—the story was largely a rehash of the incident in September. Neither there nor in a short related statement by Dr. Vincent Cooper was there any mention of a call approximately twenty-five minutes before the murder from a man identifying himself as John Warner.

Did Hallam hope by this deliberate omission to first puzzle, then vex, and finally infuriate the killer who from a position of safety had looked forward to reading about himself in the newspapers?

With eerie precision, the telephone rang, but only to presage the arrival of an elderly rose-point Siamese with chronic kidney trouble. Belinda, who had tensed automatically, got the card from the file and went with it to the main clinic.

There, although it was eleven-thirty, she delved into her smock pocket for the piece of paper on which she had written Hallam's home phone number. The thought crossed her mind as she dialed that not only would he consider her platonic relationship with Norman unlikely, as she was sure Dr. Hilary had, but he might go a step further and speculate that Norman had tired of the affair first and so become the target of a vengeful troublemaker.

When would the liberation movement turn its zeal from chairpeople to the line about the woman scorned?

And Hallam's telephone had rung to no avail at least a dozen times, and here came a coughing golden retriever, a spotted dog whose badly inflamed footpad contained a large sliver of broken-off glass, and the promised Siamese, so horrified at these known surroundings that its eyes were violently instead of slightly crossed.

It was twelve o'clock at last. Unlike Deb, Hilda Rushmore was never early; she arrived on the dot with an airy, "Coming in the front door, just like quality!" and, to the guard, "Oh, goody."

The yellow smock displayed when she whipped off her coat became her; she was more a warm bronze than black. Belinda had never asked her how long it took to do all those stiffly dancing braids, no thicker than the average knitting needle; it must be a very tedious question.

Heading for her own locker with the door ritually secured, she went over the cases under her tutelage and then hesitated. "You didn't by any chance get a call for me after you came on last night?"

"No." Liquid eyes that could snap with merriment or irritation, but now were only brooding. "Just the one call for Deb, I couldn't swear to either a man or a woman. Could they speak to her? This must have been about two o'clock. Nobody had told me what to say, but I thought I'd better keep my mouth shut so I asked if I could take a message. And they said," Hilda had suddenly realized the inwardness, because she gripped her hands tightly together, " 'No, I don't believe so.' "

What had the voice hoped for, needed to hear? A tearful "She's been shot, she's dead"?

The very evasion, the pretense that nothing frightful had taken place at the clinic, would have served.

So someone could have an untroubled night's sleep.

"The graveyard shift can be awfully quiet. I sometimes let the cats out to play," said Hilda, anxious. "It didn't have to be . . . I mean, Deb may have a friend who checked with her off and on."

That young earnestness encouraging the frivolous use of the clinic line, even in the small hours? "Maybe," said Belinda, because the other girl looked disturbed at the thought of even a tenuous connection with a murderer. "Good-night."

The guard escorted her out, still absorbed in his studies. Did she know that in Spanish *pronto* meant *soon* instead of a hurry-up ultimatum? Belinda had not known. Even though her car was locked she was grateful for his capable bulk, his flashlight sweep of the shadowy back seat, his friendly wave as she got started.

She was all at once exhausted in every respect. After a single glance at the German shepherd with the porcupine quills Dr. Hilary had asked the stalwart owner if he would mind staying to transport it from table to run, but the Labrador, even though not full-grown, had been heavier than it looked. Belinda pressed her shoulders back against the seat, trying to arch away some of the ache, and glanced up and saw the headlights behind her.

In what she had accepted as complete security she wasn't in the habit of monitoring the rear-view mirror, but it was her impression that this stretch of night driving, with the gas station and a fast-food place left behind, had always been unaccompanied. Still, the road had not been built for the exclusive after-midnight use of Belinda Grace. Even when she turned right onto Currant Road and the headlights followed, it didn't mean that Norman was at the wheel.

And if he was?

Belinda was well aware that where Norman was concerned her brain did not function with real lucidity. She hadn't gotten across to Dr. Hilary, and it was difficult if not impossible to explain even to Zari, the sinking dread that was mixed with her simpler fear, the conviction that he had the ability to destroy her. By the smashing of her confidence he had already propelled her from one world into another; but he could go further than that.

An analyst would probably have said that she was subconsciously blaming Norman for the actual and potent virus that had begun its successful invasion of her system well before his pretended suicide. If there was an element of truth in that, it was so fractional as not to matter. There had been alarm signals earlier, when she was perfectly well, but she had ignored them out of loyalty, or, less commendably, a refusal to believe that she was wrong and everybody else was right.

See Norman, coaxed the imaginary analyst—in some public place if you're worried about physical safety. Tell him calmly and firmly that any further contact with him is out of the question. Slay the dragon.

But that was why some people wore medical-identification bracelets: to guard against any exposure to a drug or other element that had produced such a violent reaction that a second incident could prove dangerous or even fatal. Belinda's bracelet would have been inscribed, "Do not expose to Norman Comstock."

And her mirror was now black and empty. While she had been concentrating on a narrow but treacherously deep fissure in the road, the headlights behind her had vanished.

Three minutes later she was home. The house was dark except for the fan-lit front hall and the curtained warmth of

Donald Aintree's windows. Belinda locked the car, whose roof light hadn't functioned for months, and, in the cone of radiance outside the front door, began to search for her key.

A classic mistake; she knew it too late.

From somewhere in the near distance there was an engine hum, coming closer. Having circled quietly through lanes and side streets so as to approach from the other direction, nothing whatever to do with Belinda until . . . ?

Frantically, she pressed Donald Aintree's button.

As swiftly as if she had communicated her panic by way of a scream, the door release sounded, and she was safely inside with a lock behind her. Donald Aintree stood against the lamp-lit background of his living room.

"I'm sorry, I couldn't find my key, but it must be here some—" The true nature of her situation struck Belinda with such force that her voice shook to a stop.

"Come in," said Donald Aintree, putting out an unhurried hand as if to someone frozen on a roof edge, "and sit down. You don't," he smiled at her with grave apology, "look quite ready for the stairs."

It was a pleasant room, thought Belinda, fastening her attention deliberately outward as she was more or less led to a chair, its ivory walls largely unbothered except by up-rushing lamplight, a bull's-eye mirror whose gilded frame was dark with age, a few pen-and-inks.

Her unwitting host had vanished with a rapid, "I'll be right back," and there was time to absorb the fact that the functions of three rooms were combined here, somehow without crowding. There was an old coppery couch, a handsome wing chair with only hints of color left in its brocade, a desk with covered typewriter, and an uncompromising straight chair, bookcases, and, near what would be the doorway to the kitchen, a small dining table.

A safe place, with a deep, almost measurable tranquility. Belinda could feel her panic sudsiding like water into sand.

"Here you are." Aintree put a short icy bubble glass into her hand, carried his own beer to the wing chair, and studied her strange forward perch. "Aren't you . . . ? Oh." He got up, crossed to the couch, picked up one of its inside and bolsterlike cushions, and tucked it behind Belinda's back. "Better?"

"Yes, thank you." Owing to the Labrador's weight, she had been afraid of snapping in half in the armchair's depth. Wise to explain; he might be able to help her in at least one way, but not if he thought her altogether lunatic. "I had to carry a dog at work and he turned out to be very heavy."

"Carrying dogs. They ought to be ashamed of themselves," said Aintree, light with her, giving her time.

The mirror was at such an angle that Belinda could see herself in it: total pallor except for the remains of her lipstick, distraught eyes with the beginning of blue under them. No wonder that, without asking, he had given her what turned out to be Scotch with only a civilized amount of water. At this rate, she would have to join A.A.

She said, "I'm sorry to have—" and at the same instant he said, "Something's frightening you, isn't it? I mean apart from the girl at the clinic?"

Long breath. "A man I don't want to see has followed me here from Boston. He was only a friend, but he seems to have thought—" Leave it at that; she had done enough detailing for Dr. Hilary, and Hallam's detached appraisal of her folly still lay ahead. "I wondered if you had noticed a car parked along here very recently."

Because until she knew what kind of vehicle Norman was driving she could be taken by surprise at any time. Tail-gating, dangerous bad manners at the best of times, would seem to contain a personal threat, especially after dark.

It was entirely possible that Norman was now miles away, having accomplished his objective and content to leave her with just these reflections, along with a new fear of the telephone; but that was a chance Belinda dared not take.

"A man did park a little way up from the corner yesterday afternoon, early, but I don't know how long he stayed because Mrs. Calvacaressi blew another fuse. I think she makes toast while she irons. He seemed to be studying a road map—well, naturally. If I'm remembering properly," said Donald Aintree, gazing at the floor in a concentrating way, "it was a silver-gray compact."

Belinda's heart sank. Silver gray had so dominated the automotive industry the year before that it accounted for perhaps three out of ten cars, and compacts were the rule rather than the exception. As a description, it bordered on the useless.

"There were reflections all over the windshield. . . . What does he look like, for future reference?"

Belinda told him, hearing herself with a sharp, belated dismay. Was it something she had heard one of the vets observe in a medical context, or did it go back to the first exchange of grunts in a cave?

No matter; it was done, and in her intermittent delving she had found her keys. An enormously savory odor was creeping out of the kitchen—Donald Aintree's drink-making errand had included putting something on a stove burner—and now he said, "Dog carrying is hungry work, and now that you're here and while you're not on your feet," he smiled at her, "won't you stay and have some chicken hash? It's hot."

Comfort emanated from him, absolute, as dangerous to Belinda as an innocent-looking little white pill because she could easily come to lean on it and in essence leaning was something she had to do by herself. Did he even believe—doubt came worming in, chilly—that she had not fled a sultry, complicated affair? She was not, demonstrably, the best judge of men.

"It smells heavenly, but I've kept you long enough," she said, standing with only a single bolt of lightning through her lower back. "Thank you for the drink, and for taking me in. Good-night."

She left her harbor, and it had been that. She didn't glance behind her as she started up the stairs. Her nerves woke up again, pointing out to her the heavy old rose curtain at the back of the landing that bisected the house.

"Fire escape," Zari had said, sweeping velvet folds away from a glass door further protected by a storm door, which opened on a small platform and had steps going down. "Key in lock at all times, and failing that, this pretty axe. Actually, I don't think anybody would come to too much harm just dropping out of a window."

Even though she knew such an action to bring together a spark and a fan, Belinda parted the curtain and tested the knob above the key. The door was locked.

She let herself into the apartment, switched on lamps, turned on bath water, put the pot of clam chowder she had made the morning before over a very low flame. The telephone rang.

Zari? Hallam, returning her call after having checked with the station? Or balked Norman, whom she was not up to facing tonight?

Belinda turned off her bath. She let the phone ring thirteen times, which seemed a wearing-down effort on the part of whoever held the receiver at the other end, and when it had finally fallen silent she dialed the Boston apartment. As she had expected, there was no answer.

A long soak in hot water and then a dinner of chowder with airy Portuguese bread brought a measure of relaxation. Belinda was in bed, her muscles recovered, when her treacherous brain told her why, in the middle of describing Norman to Donald Aintree, she had been visited by that pang of doubt.

Dr. Kitsch, explaining to a client why he would not do a biopsy on a Great Pyrenees, too old for major surgery, with a suspect growth. Belinda had not been listening closely, because unlike Deb Kingsley she had no plans for making this a life work, but there had been something about a contained malignancy.

To Dr. Hilary, Norman was as blank as an unstamped key.

To Donald Aintree he was physically identifiable. Confidences tended to unravel in all directions, particularly the one you hadn't looked in. Had she, in some way she could not define, turned the malignancy loose?

# Chapter
# Eleven

"Where in Pennsylvania?" In the tarnish-colored morning Hallam's gaze was brilliant with speculation.

Once again Belinda seemed to hold Norman's driver's license in a hand unsteady with refusal. He looked implacably back at her from the glossy surface, his then shorter hair turned unfamiliarly dark by the camera, the contours of his face altered by a complying smile. Why did they always want that smile? People with their licenses summarily demanded of them were seldom grinning ear to ear.

She said, "Bell Falls."

Hallam made his third abbreviated note. "It won't do any harm to see if they're interested."

The sharp line he drew across his notebook page had a somewhat dismissive air, and Belinda realized that his tightrope attention had not been for her at all. He had obviously listened, interrupting once to inquire how Norman could have discovered her presence in Pippin, but somehow had reduced the tiger to a prowling tomcat supplied unwisely with saucers of milk. She ought to have felt relieved, because theoretically he was versed in such matters, but it was a little like taking a plunge into what was only an inch deep.

Or was that part of the general strangeness of the morning? She had finally slept the way people do when they seek sanctuary, deeply and without dreaming except for one clear and astonishing flash. Hallam's call at ten o'clock, returning hers of the evening before, had dragged her awake to such a cold and thunderous dimness that now, at not quite eleven, there were lamps lit in the living room.

Thus illumined at such an odd hour, a seascape of Zari's with polished sun fragmented on long, green rollers had the calmly disorienting effect of a window on a totally foreign climate. On top of that was a different quality in Hallam from the moment he entered: a combined simmer, tension, triumph.

Belinda herself had felt slightly bemused even after a second mug of coffee. As if the dream—although not really that; a single scene, a single question answered by a glance—had been a developing agent, she knew who Donald Aintree was.

Barring unlikely coincidence, he had written *The Christmas Tour*, a soberly antic novel in which, through a series of doomed misunderstandings, the wrong house was invaded as part of a charity project organized by a group of important matrons. Here, instead of the splendid furnishings presided over by hostess-gowned wife and smoking-jacketed husband, were cobwebs, sprung cushions, people given to drink and currently harboring a talented parrot being held for ransom.

The biographical note had been pithy: "D. J. Aintree lives in Pippin, Mass., where he does not sail."

Hallam said with a recalling abruptness, "This isn't for publication, but the lab found a couple of dog hairs, black-tipped brown, on the strip of rug Deborah put down after you left. The rug had apparently just been washed along with something linty, like a towel, but the lint had gone deep into the fiber. The hairs were on the surface."

Black and brown: the shepherd cross. Belinda did not have

to be told that pet owners often carried hairs about with them, but wouldn't the rain have provided an adhesiveness?

Not on the underside of a coat sleeve, or in the case of a rushing, buffeting wind.

"So," said Hallam, "until we can trace the dog—and Tex isn't a popular name around here, so far we've only found two and they're both ruled out—let's have a crack at the man." He smiled at Belinda for the first time. "It really isn't impossible."

From the outset it was plain that he was used to dredging information from people convinced that they didn't possess it. Instead of confronting Belinda with questions about coloring and features, he started off on an apparent tangent.

"The temperature was in the low twenties until it warmed up a bit for the rain. When he began to alter the wording on the release form, did he take off a glove?"

Without effort or warning a bare hand presented itself, red with cold and fisted around the chained pen as if this were an unaccustomed exercise, which only wrath was making him undertake. Belinda said surprisedly, "No," and described the thick fingers with little tufts of sandy hair on the backs, noticeable under the pour of fluorescent light.

Hallam was pleased but did not try to force her to any conclusions. "Hat?"

"I think so, but I have no idea what kind."

"You were standing pretty close to him. Did you get the impression that he'd been drinking?"

" . . . No." Again by oblique suggestion, the obvious source of fumes was conjured up. "But he had one of those thin, longish mouths that don't ever open very wide."

Hallam did not share Belinda's amazement at her drop-by-drop release of memory. "You've had this all along, sandwiched in between a couple of unpleasant incidents and then a shock. And it's inhibiting when a physical description may be crucial. . . . You guessed his age at fifty or fifty-five. Did you get that from gait, or paunch, or eye bags?"

But for all his low-key expertise, the faucet was abruptly turned off. Belinda, trying to force recollection when no force had been needed earlier, said at last, "The fact that he was so red, I suppose, although that could have been the wind instead of high blood pressure."

Hallam considered her for a moment and then stood up, walking a few steps away from the softening lamplight. At the window he said, "How old would you say I am?"

Belinda gazed up at him, taking in the seacoast skin that did not turn winter pale, a touch of crinkling at the corners of the dark gray eyes, the experienced mouth. "Thirty-seven, thirty-eight."

"Not bad," said Hallam, and then with one of his curious lapses, "And you're what, twenty-five?"

Belinda was not to be outdone in circumspection. "Thereabouts."

His gaze stayed inquisitively on her face. At her expression when the telephone rang he said matter-of-factly, "That may be for me."

It was. Belinda, carrying the coffee mugs to the kitchen, assured herself that the man they were trying to reconstruct had no matching interest in her. Since he could not know that she had destroyed his card without his name or address registering, he would assume by this time that she had either forgotten his existence or passed the information along to the police, who weren't interested. In any case she did not have the vulnerability of a lone tree in a flat landscape. Dr. Cooper had seen and talked to him too, if only for seconds.

There was a third possibility: that while official attention was being focused on a boor who went through life venting his spleen on postal clerks and garage mechanics and anyone else who did not leap at the snap of his fingers, the actual killer was sitting tranquilly at home with the Sunday paper.

Postponing the pleasure, prolonging the anticipation, of picking up the telephone, dialing, saying another, "Hello, Belinda dear"?

Suppose he had acquired Norman Comstock's driver's license and other identification, suppose Norman Comstock reposed in a cemetery somewhere?

The mug Belinda had finished washing ended up in a splintering crash on the floor. Hallam, appearing in the doorway, retrieved the handle, which had flown at his feet, and put it on the counter as if it might someday be useful. "Two more dogs named Tex," he said. "Does either Pierce or Burack ring a bell?"

He was undiscouraged by the shake of Belinda's head. "We'll have a look. Will you be available for the next half hour or so, just in case?"

"Yes." Although she had planned to do a more comprehensive grocery shopping than usual; the sky seemed to call for it. "How do you . . . ? Can the police just descend?"

"Simple." Hallam put on the coat he had slung over his arm. "Child in the neighborhood bitten by dog so we're making a house-to-house check in the hope of avoiding the painful rabies shots and so forth. On the weekend, we got to see all the inhabitants."

"You didn't by any chance call here late last night, did you?"

"No, last night I was—" Hallam, at the door, cut that off sharply, studied Belinda, summed up what lay behind the question. "It could have been for your friend, you know, someone she forgot to tell about the switch of apartments."

It was reasonable. It was also, from his tone, like a kindly pat on the head for an importunate child. Belinda, locking the door, thought stoically that she could not make anyone understand the wrecker capacity in Norman.

With the possible exception of Donald Aintree.

Seen in a mirror in a tiny whip of time while she slept. Her name had been mentioned inquiringly, and he had turned on the unseen speaker a glance of such private joy and possessiveness that it brought her awake.

Even in her startlement in the darkened bedroom, that hadn't been difficult to figure out. She had been panicked by one man, and another and very attractive man had given her shelter, calm, a feeling of utter security. Her bruised confidence had subconsciously translated that into a genuine reluctance to let her go.

A half hour or so, Hallam had said. Belinda swept up the fragments of pottery and settled herself to wait.

Late the night before, Hallam had dedicated himself to some unusual and deliberate drinking. Peculiarly enough, as if the intake had really been therapeutic, he had opened his eyes without a trace of hangover.

Earlier, although the prices were almost sufficient for a small down payment on a lobster boat, he had taken himself to Wycoff's, justly famed along the coast for its shore dinners. As Sue had not liked seafood, it held no memories for either good or ill.

All the more shock, then, to look up and see her being conducted past his table, followed by a dark man, zestfully sideburned, who in spite of expensive tailoring was following his own stomach. The waiter seated them directly across from Hallam, Sue on the banquette facing the room. As if noticing him for the first time, although she had had command from the entrance, she gave him a self-possessed little wave and presently murmured to her companion.

Twenty seconds, Hallam told himself, and it was exactly that before the dark man turned his head for an idly thorough inspection. Hallam could think of no reason to nod by way of acknowledgment, and gave him back stare for stare.

It was the first time he had seen Sue since the stony meeting in the lawyer's office; she had gone to her parents' in Ipswich for the duration of the divorce proceedings. He tried to arm himself detachedly by searching for whatever had attracted him in the first place, and it was all still there: shine of hair, curve of cheek, buoyant statement that the world was new and she loved every bit of it.

I have met the enemy, and she is someone else's.

Hallam's second drink came, and presently his dinner. It was never entirely satisfactory to consume boiled lobster under an eye that might be considered very watchful, and that was when he ordered a third, although this was his ritual time for draft beer. A double, so as to save the waiter steps.

Sue, who had always denounced both clams and oysters as gray and grisly, addressed herself briskly to a plate of steamers. Hallam could not help noticing that, and the occasional stroke she gave to the fur muff on the banquette beside her, as if with sufficient encouragement it might get up and begin to walk around.

A muff. By that association, he was back at the scene of the final quarrel.

After a long hot day, disastrous in every respect, he got home to find that the household of three dogs, two cats, and a crow with a lopsided wing had been augmented by what seemed to be an overweight eel but turned out to be a cringing dachshund. Hallam maintained his control until he had showered and made gin and tonics, and then he said, "Sue, honey, we cannot adopt every—"

"I found him in the middle of the traffic on Front Street and he's still terrified. Just look at his eyes."

Hallam looked at his eyes, which were indeed bolting out of fear or possibly accustomed guilt. Next he looked at the mail. In it, unnoticed by Sue or she would have put it aside for a more propitious moment, was a thirty-dollar veterinary bill for the cleaning of one of the cats' teeth.

The cat in question, Georgiana, was barely out of kittenhood, and if he had thought about it at all Hallam would not have expected feline dental expenses for some time. The crow chose to utter a loud and grating caw, which sounded derisive. Hallam clung to his temper like a drowning man. "This has gotten ridiculous, Sue. If you fed those animals the proper—"

"It's preventive hygiene," said Sue, swiftly on the attack. "You eat properly, but you have your teeth cleaned."

The total inanity of this reduced Hallam to a similar level. "Yes, but I don't send the bill to the cat."

Sue departed to the kitchen, scooping up Georgiana on the way as though Hallam, left alone with it, might tear the cat's head off. She was gone a long time, and when she reappeared she was freshly powdered around the eyes. "Your dinner is on the table, Charles. I—"

Hallam forestalled her with a lifted forefinger, which might have looked roguish from a distance. "Let me guess. You have a headache."

But he was not a quarrelsome man or a grudge bearer, and for the rest of the evening he made excuses for Sue. She was an only child, born when her parents were in their forties and scarcely knew what to do with her. As a result, they had showered her with pets, which were their intermediaries and her outlet for affection.

Here a sensible voice in Hallam's head observed: a dog. All right, two dogs, to be company for each other when Sue was out, and maybe a cat not on a diet of baby food—but everything that moves?

He disregarded the voice. When he had let all hands except the crow out and then in again, he tiptoed into the silent bedroom, slid quietly under the coverlet, reached out a hand to Sue, and was bitten smartly by the dachshund snuggled between them.

That had been seven months ago. Hallam had not confided to anyone his bitter conviction that there were people to whom pets, and in time any animals, became as dangerously addictive as gambling or alcohol. A warp in the accepted priorities came about, with a sacrificing of the human element.

Divorce in such cases must be common enough even though at the time he had felt singled out. How far might the obsession go, given a dovetailing of circumstances? Unlike cats, dogs were an extension of the owner's personality. Suppose a man were to have imagined not only a rejection but a rejection of life-threatening proportions?

Hallam was careful not to deny to himself that he was out to prove a private hypothesis; even an inner defense implied an awareness of a conceivable accusation from without. Still, as he drove up to the first of the two addresses passed along to him by Sergeant Uffi, who had then gone off to take a deposition in connection with another case, he felt a familiar tight sensation.

Coming close.

On the far side of town, Joanne Wishart took her billowing laundry off the line, heard the telephone begin to ring, called her Yorkshire terrier and, puffing a little, let them both back into the warm kitchen.

"Hello?" Then, after the first few words through the receiver, "Oh, yes, you called yesterday but there was someone at your door. Sorry I haven't been available since, my mother's broken her hip and I'm over there most of the time, but I did finally find the name. I knew I'd made a note of it somewhere because I'm convinced they give the puppy a better home if they know they're on record. Hold on . . ."

Over the years, out of a firm if erroneous belief that the surgery made them lazy and fat, Joanne Wishart had never had her female dogs spayed. When her various security measures failed, which happened surprisingly seldom, she house-trained the puppies—no matter what the mixture, they were dears when they were tiny—and then, if she could not find ready takers, she put them in a large cardboard box and was at the animal shelter a few minutes after it opened. But not inside.

It was a very successful maneuver. People arriving in search of a pet seemed to feel that they were pulling off a coup by acquiring one directly from a car, as indeed they were with no adoption fee involved, and the sight of one person driving happily away with a puppy generated enthusiasm among other comers. The shelter, of course, remained in ignorance.

Joanne was aware that she broke all kinds of statutes, but she could not bring herself to abandon trusting puppies to possible doom—almost certain in the case of her Yorkshire terrier's strange-looking pair of offspring, long-haired dachshunds from the neck on.

Now there was this terminally ill little boy in Swampscott, whose dog had been killed by a speeding motorist. He didn't know it; he had been told that the dog was at the vet's. There were other children in the family, and the emotionally taxed parents could not go combing around for an exact lookalike.

The caller, a concerned neighbor, had happened to be in Pippin, spotted a matching dog in a parked car, made inquiries, learned that the actual owner was in Florida, but persevered in getting Miss Wishart's name in the hope that there was a littermate. Needless to say, the caller would buy the puppy from its present owners.

Joanne, not pausing to consider the unlikelihood of all this, thought, gratified, to herself: And they say there's no kindness left in the world.

She returned to the telephone. "Here you are—do you have a pencil?"

# Chapter
# Twelve

When Hattie put on her coat at a few minutes before noon, Roger bent himself into S-curves of wagging expectancy, but when she said, "Mind the house," he went immediately to sit under the dining room table. The cat, stretched on a chair, gave him an idle cuff as he passed, but he paid no attention. This was his maltreated posture since being deprived of his run, and he wanted Hattie to get the full benefit of it.

She wavered. What with dinner at the Farrises', Roger would spend a good part of the evening by himself. He loved the car and was a good passenger, sitting sedately on the seat beside her and only standing occasionally to gaze at the great world.

Moreover, she had only two errands: her unfailing Sunday lunchtime visit to an elderly man, one of her last patients and now confined to a wheelchair, and a brief supermarket stop. The trouble was her slightly bent key, returned to her in that state by Peter Farris, who had borrowed the Buick in some unremembered emergency, with an airy, "You need graphite in those locks."

Sometimes the key worked, but sometimes it was difficult to the point of impossibility. Hattie had a spare set, but she had obviously not put them in a cubbyhole of the living room desk as she thought because now, when she went to look, they weren't there.

The prospect of leaving the car unlocked with her charge in it during her short absences had not troubled Hattie until today. Pippin was not a high-crime town; she had no tape decks or other obvious targets; Front Street, where her ex-patient dwelt, had a good deal of both pedestrian and motor traffic even on Sundays.

But, since his digging out of his run and his hours of liberty, she had to look upon Roger as a plotter and an escaper. Juveniles with nothing better to do often sped by on bicycles, yanking down the flaps of mailboxes. If one of them tested a door of the Buick out of idle mischief, just to see if it was open, Roger would not stay to guard the car; he would be out in a twinkling.

Among the busy wheels; not nearly as visible as a big dog.

Hattie could almost hear the cut-off shriek of brakes applied in vain, and then—hastily, she blacked out the immediate scene—her necessary call to Bernard Odom. "Something terrible has happened . . ."

Her stewardship over, when it was only well begun. While professing commiseration, the people concerned would say, and rightly, "*Everybody* locks cars these days."

It came to Hattie with surprise that, independent of any other consideration, she would be quite sorry to see Roger in a motionless crumple, eyes deceptively staring as if he could still see.

There was a locksmith on Front Street, and she had a vague notion that it was open on Sundays. She could have her key straightened and a duplicate set made while she brought old Mr. Worthington his dessert—brown Betty, today—and gave his parakeet's cage a new lining and did her shopping. The fence man was due on Tuesday, and with the run in operation again all would be as before.

Meanwhile, Hattie bent under the table to glance at Roger's wilted face. "Play with Whitey," she said coaxingly, "and I'll take you for a walk when I come home."

Falling over backward, she thought as she left the driveway. But, and she did not dream of her irony, better be safe than sorry.

After giving instructions as to how to get to Westmorland Drive, Hallam had said, "You might want to alter your appearance a bit." Belinda, hanging up, viewed this as an understatement.

She had sometimes wondered about the reluctance of witnesses to identify suspects in murder trials; now she knew. Apart from the natural fear of making what might prove to be a giant mistake and the equally natural fear of reprisal, there was a deep unease about taking a step into the world of a total stranger, making footprints that could not be called back.

Accordingly, she dressed as if for her other life. Classic pumps instead of the flats that she wore for speedy and soundless progress on the clinic's tile floors. Her midnight-blue coat, fitted and gently skirted, collar turned up in back to cup her head. The nubbly, pearly pull-on hat. Crystal studs at her ears to catch rainbowy points of light.

This unfamiliar reflection—someone sure, unworried, looking forward to an intriguing encounter—was locked in the mirror inside the bedroom closet door. Belinda was closing the door when her gaze dropped and stopped. She finished the closure with infinite care.

A clear feminine voice, a trifle high, cut itself off as she appeared at the top of the stairs. The girl with Donald Aintree in the lower hall turned to follow his lifted gaze.

She had been led to believe that an open inspection and weighing of people was her right if not her actual duty, and she was not pleased at Belinda's amiable smile. There was a suggestion of "Speak when you're spoken to" about the firming of her raspberry lips with their catlike upturn at the corners.

Donald Aintree performed introductions. Belinda felt a blush starting up from her throat at his glance, thought absurdly of adding "Do you glue your hair together?" to her civil greeting of cool Mrs. Laurence Aintree, reached for the doorknob, heard behind her, "Excuse me a minute, Cherry."

Outside in the cold lavender air, Donald said without any pointless apologies about spying, "I saw your official visitor this morning. Is he hectoring you?"

Kind, because she had in effect made a present of herself and her problems to him last night without being asked. Beguiling enough for a half hour or so, perhaps, because all must be grist to a writer's mill, but eventually a bore and a burden.

"No," she said with a certain light crispness. "There's a man he wants me to look at, that's all."

"Oh," said Donald.

And now she was off, in roughly the neighborhood of lunch, looking like a Christmas rose on this dark day. Could those be her suspect-identifying clothes?

Donald went back into the house to find Cherry slapping a glove against the banister although he had been gone less than the minute requested. Was it Napoleon who had complained, "I almost had to wait"?

"Très chic," she said. "Is she always that color, or do you keep the upstairs apartments terribly warm?"

The cat that wanted to eat any canary in sight. Donald, never very close to the brother who had always seemed to wear a button marked "Head of the Family," was nevertheless a little sorry for Laurence.

He said, ignoring the question, "Where were we? If Hattie weren't such a pillar of rectitude, you would be tempted to think—what?"

To the uninitiated, Westmorland Drive spoke of breadth, trees, handsome houses with sweeping lawns. Such was not the case.

Ten years earlier, when to the horror of the natives Pippin

had for a time been invaded by beautiful people, a Florida-based developer had drained a large area of marshland, put in some fill, and flung up a dozen two-bedroom houses as a pilot project. In his haste to catch the tide, so to speak, the houses were almost literally put together with staples, and the cheap white paint quickly turned a scaly gray under what the advertising brochure described evasively as "ocean breezes."

Paving was promised but never came. The marsh crept stealthily back, as anybody could have told the developer it would, and more young mountains of fill arrived to further enhance a vista of otherwise dead-flat reedy wetness and, on a clear day, billboards signifying the presence of a much larger town to the west.

Unsuccessful lawsuits were brought by enraged out-of-state buyers who had acquired their "seacoast cottages" sight unseen except for a single photograph showing an ironwork lantern, which did not come with the house, and a healthy tree in full leaf, the shot so angled that its burlapped ball of earth did not show. A stronger case might have been presented by the woman who had fallen through her tiny front porch in the first week of occupancy, but the developer had prudently vanished.

The implication, in careful phrases, had been that the properties would be an investment as rentals in the nonvacation months, but the winds blasted through them from September until April. A few owners managed to find buyers who were enthusiastic about hammers and saws and panels of sheathing; a few more found hardy, desperate tenants. The rest of the structures were vandalized and then fell gradually to pieces.

There were now five mailboxes remaining on Westmorland Drive. One of them was marked "C. McFee."

In spite of a vague dread of what amounted to a spy mission, Belinda could appreciate the advisability of her going alone. If Hallam had driven her instead of taking up a bird-watching stance at the edge of the marsh, it could be argued that in his anxiety to make an arrest in the murder of Deborah Kingsley he had pressed for a positive identification.

There he was, field glasses lowered briefly as if in expectation of another weekend naturalist before he turned away again. As planned, and in case McFee made a habit of keeping a close observation on visitors to this bleak outpost, Belinda cruised slowly along the rutted road, pausing to examine mailboxes, before she turned, drove back, and braked in front of the second house on the right.

Even under a sunless sky, the plastic-shrouded windows glistened watchfully as she left the car and entered the yard, an oblong of frozen mud bisected by a pair of wooden planks. To one side was an iron stake with a length of swivel chain attached. Near it, a water bowl contained a half-inch of ice.

*You'd better hope this dog doesn't die on me.*

Belinda's heart assumed a racketing pace as she knocked on the door. Hallam was there, and she had her new knowledge from that random glance into the bedroom closet, but this was still like undoing the final wrappings from a box with a steady ticking inside.

The door opened, and McFee stood looking at her amid an incongruous waft of frying onions. He was not as red as before, and his eyes had failed to register because their color tended to disappear into the rest of his face. In the instant that the knob began its turn she had trained her gaze on the area she was surest of, and there were the thick fingers with the aggressive tufts of sandy hair.

She had a tiny flash of stage-fright blankness, although he showed no sign of recognition. "I'm looking for some people named Fisher, this is the road they—"

The almost lipless mouth barely parted. "Never heard of them," said McFee curtly, and closed the door.

"It's the same man," said Belinda when Hallam joined her at her car, parked behind his on the track leading to Westmorland Drive, "but—" was it a devil's-advocate point, arising from the fact that McFee inspired both trepidation and dislike? "—from what I saw of the dog that night, walking normally, it's hard to believe that it died within two hours."

Hallam was there ahead of her. "Maybe he couldn't face the prospect of the night, and put it out of its misery. All the more blame for the clinic, in his mind."

And then, gun still in hand while he gazed at the body of the dog, flamed up all over again at the memory of being turned away. . . . He didn't look like a man of either affection or sentiment, but a belligerent possessiveness could be stronger than either.

It was so believable that Belinda felt bound to tell Hallam her chance discovery at once. "About the hairs on the rug. I found a black and brown one on the slacks I was wearing Friday night, just before I left for here, and I didn't come in direct contact with the dog at all."

Which could mean that air currents had been responsible for what had seemed like evidence of McFee's return after midnight.

A sudden flight of gulls came wheeling and crying overhead to fill up the silence in which the whole afternoon had jerked to a halt. Belinda found herself grateful for them. Hallam said with perfect courtesy, "That was very observant of you. I'd better come and get it for comparison."

He followed her back to the house and, in Zari's bedroom, labeled an envelope and placed the hair inside. Something about his very meticulousness suggested that this was in no way going to interfere with his pursuit of McFee's dog, almost certainly dead, conceivably of a bullet that would match the two that mattered.

Belinda said, deliberately testing, "I called Zari. Norman Comstock has gone without leaving a forwarding address."

"Oh?" Envelope slipping neatly into pocket. "When?"

"Sometime between Wednesday afternoon and Friday morning, when his landlady got back from visiting a relative. She told Zari he'd been talking about Bennington, Vermont."

"From what I gather, I think he'd fit in very well in Bennington," said Hallam. "Seriously. He could read his poetry aloud in coffeehouses to the creative writing majors, and possibly poetry majors too. Come to that, he might have called you from Vermont. With direct dialing—"

As if blips had been picked up on a private screen, the telephone rang. Hallam and Belinda exchanged a glance and he came to stand close, listening as she answered it to a woman's voice saying, "Zari? I'll give you three guesses who this—" Doubtful, belated pause. "This is Zari, isn't it?"

Belinda, unsure as to how Zari would feel about being located by someone who wanted her identity guessed at, passed along the Boston number and nothing more. Hallam said, "While you're at it, why don't you give the clinic a ring? McFee may have cooled down and brought his dog in since you were there."

It was clear that he didn't really think so, and neither did Belinda, and they were both right. He was starting to button his coat when something stopped him visibly short. He took out his notebook instead, flipped through pages, paused to read, flipped again, paused again.

He said, "According to Deborah's brother," thank God he doesn't call her Kingsley, thought Belinda in a removed way, "she nearly hit a dog on the afternoon before she was killed, and had a few angry words with the owner. Two different men, two different dogs? Or the same pair?"

He stared through Belinda, who was remembering guiltily that she had forgotten to tell him about Deb's indignation over the near miss. It hadn't seemed to have any bearing then, and still didn't.

Hallam continued not to see her, brilliantly. "Didn't McFee say when he brought his dog in that it had been vomiting blood?"

"Yes."

And at last she was coming back into focus, because Hallam's face closed. Since she had presented him with the similar-sounding hair on her slacks, he was going to keep his own counsel; it was as clear as if he had spoken the words.

What he did say at the door, surprisingly in view of his

fresh preoccupation, was, "I don't think you have anything to worry about from that quarter, but I'll let you know what we turn up about Comstock."

Somewhere, Norman heard him.

Belinda was making a survey of refrigerator and shelves for purposes of shopping when the telephone rang, and not in the checked and then start-again signal she had arranged with Zari while she waited the agreed length of time for Hallam.

She lifted the receiver, braced, knowing that it was imperative not to hide for at least this one occasion. Norman's voice, smooth and pleasant and unfathomably dangerous, said, "Belinda. I'm glad you got back all right."

It was a cold splash rather than a drench, thanks to her preparedness; even so, her breathing wasn't quite ready.

"When do you expect your parents back?" asked Norman, conversational.

As if, staggeringly, he had the right to a cozy interest in the activities of the Grace family. Never a tiger after all, thought Belinda, but a badger, refusing to give up the prey into which it had sunk its formidable teeth.

Unless—and it was the only thing that made sense of his astonishing approach—she consented to a wiping out of what had happened, and a restoration of the old companionable footing long enough to demonstrate to her friends and family that she had been wrong and was now repentant. Then he might relax his jaw, let her go, depart to dig himself another run somewhere.

"You just missed a man who's extremely interested in you," she said, surprised at the steadiness of her voice but unable to address him by name. "A police lieutenant, as a matter of fact."

"Really? I would have thought they'd have their hands full with more pressing matters. I certainly hope they're keeping a guard at the clinic," said Norman, and hung up.

Belinda left the apartment precipitately. Even if her larder had been equipped for a blizzard, although the sky looked too implacable for snow, she would have had to get away from what was like the seep of carbon monoxide.

She drove into town. When she had parked and left her car a block from the only market that was open on Sunday, there was a rip of lightning, a crack of thunder, an onslaught of hail that was almost golf-ball-sized, frightening in its strike, violently rebounding.

She ducked into the first shelter that offered, the recessed doorway of Benj. Wells, Locksmith, already occupied by an elderly woman in a tweed coat and a sensible felt hat. For all her bared nerve ends, she had no sense whatever of an impulse, far more guided than lightning, about to make the jump across two parallel lines.

# Chapter
# Thirteen

"Hattie. What are you doing out in this rotten weather?" Peter Farris, about to pass the doorway, checked himself and squeezed in.

Hattie turned from the nice girl with whom she had somehow fallen into conversation about the bleached spot on the front of her suit jacket. "Having my car key straightened and some others made," she said forthrightly.

She did not care much for Nan's husband, and not only because she suspected from something the usually discreet Charlotte had once let drop that he was the author of friction in that marriage. She supposed that he could be called attractive, with his very fair skin and almost classical features, but to her it was a schemer's face, the eyes as light and as gauging as mercury. His somewhat aggressive chin had a slight cleft, as if to disarm. Hattie considered him capable of having had the cleft put there, judiciously.

"And I take it that Roger," Farris nodded along the street

in the direction of the untenanted Buick, "elected to stay home with a bone and a good book?"

"More or less." His gaze, Hattie noted, was all over the girl, who after a small, polite smile was devoting her attention to the white slash and bounce of the continuing hail.

"You haven't forgotten about us?"

"No, I'm looking forward," said Hattie, although since she had answered her own naive curiosity she was not.

"Good, we'll see you." With a final silvery and devouring glance Farris loped off, his rakishly angled navy wool watch cap giving him a peculiarly—and deliberately?—undergraduate air. He was two years younger than Nan, and although she took meticulous, successful care of her face and figure the age differential seemed to be spreading.

Hattie turned to her companion, feeling that her gloved hands made it ambiguous as to whether she had an eccentric husband awaiting her return. "My name is Hattie Callahan. I hope you gathered that Roger is my dog."

"Mine is Belinda Grace, and yes, I did. You know, what would be much better than dye for your suit is pastel chalk, because you could blend it."

"Oh, what a good idea, and I think the newspaper store has them." Outside of sickrooms and the harmless diversion of putting young doctors through their paces, Hattie had always been tentative about herself. "I don't usually tell my problems to strangers, but you look good at coping."

"Not very," said the girl with a surprisingly wry curve of the lips. "I hope it works."

The hail was turning itself off although the sidewalks still stirred with bobbly white, and people began to emerge from other shelters. It seemed to Hattie a sparse trickle for Front Street until she remembered that there was a much-touted football game on television, the kind where the camera panned into the stands and found faces from Washington and Broadway and Hollywood.

She said a warm good-bye to Belinda Grace—chance interludes of spontaneous liking were few and far between—and set off in search of pastels.

Belinda did her grocery shopping in a state of such inattentiveness that later she was to find herself in possession of a package of frozen okra.

When as a result of a friendly query as to whether she was new in Pippin it came out that Donald Aintree was a relative of the tweed-coated woman with whom she shared the doorway, Belinda had been as startled as if an invisible hand had touched her shoulder. Coincidence, but coaxing her insensibly toward another of the mistakes to which she was prone?

She would have to do something about that, she thought, too bemused to check the mirror from time to time as she drove home over roads edged with heavy white lace. Zari was in no hurry to alter the existing arrangement—she had been to dinner and the theater twice with Jeb Moulton; did Belinda mind? Not in the least—but now that Norman knew exactly where to find her the Steptoe house was no safer than the Boston apartment.

Yes, it was. It had Donald Aintree on its ground floor, calmly vigilant.

Belinda veered away from that. As things stood, Hallam might well summon her back here, and in any case her paycheck was not due until Wednesday. In the meantime, snip the dream out of her memory like an unflattering photograph of herself, thereby control her tendency to blush, let Donald know that she had withdrawn any claim to his protection.

And she was not—the determination startled her by its intensity—a psychological cripple, a practiced eater of sympathy.

When she pulled into the driveway, Donald was on a ladder, taping cardboard over a section of fanlight broken by the hail.

"No great loss, the original glass was gone long ago," he said to Belinda's lifted and inquiring gaze, and descended.

"Have you had lunch? I'm starving; will you come with me and do something about that? I know, you have to be at work at four, but I know a good quick place."

It seemed an invitation extended by fate. "I'd like to," said Belinda. "About five minutes?"

Upstairs, putting away the perishables before she consulted a mirror, she discovered the okra, a vegetable which after a single encounter she had avoided with the fervor of a young child fleeing sauerkraut. Offer it to Mrs. Calvacaressi, the other second-floor tenant? Cook it and put it out for some truly desperate bird?

Donald headed toward the harbor, today dark and sullen, empty of life except for the tireless seagulls. "Did you do your identification or whatever it was?" he asked lightly, and when Belinda said that she had, "The police must be fairly sure of him, then."

For the police, read Hallam. Belinda's disquiet over McFee, the exactly square peg for the square hole, came filtering back.

"They're certainly interested," she said. Now, remind them both that she understood thoroughly why they were together in this car, lunch-bound, and be brisk and independent about it. "Norman telephoned about an hour and a half ago, and I told him they were interested in him, too."

Even gazing through the windshield she caught the sharp swing of Donald's head. When he had negotiated a corner of almost paint-scraping tightness he said, "That should give him something to think about," but it had clearly not been his initial reaction. "What was the object of the call, or was it just another 'Belinda dear'?"

The faintest of shivers, unconnected with Norman, traveled over her skin. "He wanted to know when my parents would be back from Europe."

Donald had brought the car to a halt in front of a big Colonial house whose rear windows would look directly down on the water. "Not to set off any alarms, is someone looking after the house in—where did you say, Bedlington?"

"The local police know they're away," which would mean, Belinda suspected, only a casual slowing of a patrol car on its routine rounds, "and so does a neighbor, and there's a woman who dusts and opens and closes the curtains and moves the car now and then."

"That ought to be safe enough. Besides," said Donald acutely, "just as justice must not only be done but be seen to be done, Norman would want you to have a box seat for anything he did there, and I take it you have no idea of going down there alone in the immediate future."

"None whatever," said Belinda.

The restaurant, crowded at even this relatively late hour, was devoid of quaintness. Its bare floorboards were creaky, its gracefully proportioned windows unadorned. In a purely practical way, chandeliers had replaced what would normally have been light reflected off the harbor.

Donald had evidently called ahead, because he was greeted by a beaming waiter who led them past a few discontentedly staring couples on benches to a window table and whipped out a pad at once.

"I did a stretch of bartending here last fall," said Donald offhandedly to Belinda, "and I hope they're as honest as I was." When he had ordered his martini, Belinda's bloody mary and the roast beef sandwiches he had recommended in the interest of speed, he sent his gray-blue glance upward. "I should let you know, Max, that the lady is also an ex-bartender."

The waiter gave Belinda a ceremonious little bow. "I could see that at once, sir."

By way of civil divorcement, and in order to relinquish a flashing, small-hours image of this man to which she was not entitled, it was not going as planned. Belinda said, redeploying her briskness, "I hadn't put two and two together last night. I enjoyed *The Christmas Tour* immensely."

"Did you?" Donald looked inordinately, dwellingly pleased. "From their jacket photographs, your parents must be the Graces whose last book saved me from a so-called Viennese restaurant in London where the host not only wears leather shorts but sings, or so I'm told.''

The drinks came, and due notice had been taken of Donald's bland warning; they were authoritative. "I met a relative of yours in town today," said Belinda, taking a further plunge onto a no-nonsense basis. "A Miss Callahan. She seemed very nice.''

"Hattie. She is very nice. I don't really know why . . .'' Donald rubbed his forehead with long precise fingers, abandoned that gesture, lifted his glass and put it down again, eyes going so crystally intent that they sheared the strange gay mood to pieces.

He said, "Tell me, did she have her dog with her?''

In accordance with the television schedule, Eloise Ripley had prepared Sunday's ritual midday dinner early for her family, so that at not much after two-thirty she was alone in the kitchen with a mountain of dishes and the sober, well-gravied baby in its high chair.

At the moment, the baby's regard was the only domestic one she could have borne. The mere thought of what she had done forty minutes earlier, under the covering television roar from the living room, made her heart race with triumph, because for once she had acted for herself, and fear, because her husband could be violent tempered.

Herb Ripley was a man upon whom certain principles had been stamped like a die coming down on unwitting metal. One principle was, "I'll do the providing around here," even before the advent of the shackling baby and although as a house painter he was frequently out of work thanks to either the weather or the building slump. Another was, "A boy ought to have a dog.''

Never mind that it was Eloise who had to clean up after and retrain the excited puppy, once a brief flurry of interest on the part of their six-year-old son had passed, and feed it and see that it had water. She would not have minded so much in the case of a French poodle—they had some style—or, failing that, a peke-a-poo. But, his philosopher's decision made, Herb had come home from the shelter with a dog, which, to Eloise, might almost have gone into a huge roll along with mustard and relish.

They named him Brownie. His eager face and apologetic tail made no dent on Eloise, who was a compulsive duster and vacuumer and washer and waxer of floors, and when the bitterest of the March winds were over he was banished to the yard. One of the perquisites of Herb's trade was stray lumber, and with the complaining help of his son he built a doghouse.

There Brownie slept, and thence he barked. As if mere noise might gain him readmittance to the house, he barked at children, blowing papers, kites, cats washing themselves with maddening slowness. He was a failure both as watchdog and as inculcator of responsibility, and it was only because of Herb's predictable reaction to his wife's nagging that he remained on the premises.

Now, incredibly, someone wanted to *buy* him.

Eloise, finished at the sink, advanced on the high chair with a damp washcloth. The baby squeezed its eyes shut and held its twiggy little hands out, stiff and stoical.

She had already decided on the disposition of the money; cash, she had stipulated to the miraculous voice on the telephone, to be left under the ornamental swan on the front lawn. A real beauty-shop permanent, with her hair streaked while she was about it, which Herb would accept as one of her friend Madge's more ambitious efforts. A new shower curtain to replace the present faded and cracked arrangement, and a white fake-fur coat for the baby. Any child of Eloise's, however young and once removed from the kitchen, was perfectly safe with a white coat.

She was at the foot of the stairs, baby on her hip, when Herb shouted electrifyingly, "Jackass!" He turned out to be addressing the television screen, but her heart almost stopped. With the baby tucked into its crib, she retired into the other bedroom for a nap of her own; she didn't like football and, dinner over, the evening meal would be sandwiches or frozen pizza.

The bedroom's front window looked across at a leather-working shop, closed on Sunday, and down at the swan that would soon produce its golden egg. After dark, Eloise had said, because although her husband would come around in time—a mortally sick child, after all—he mustn't know now.

Herb would go straight from football to "60 Minutes." Brownie's barking presented no problem when the time came, and neither did the gate; Herb and their son occasionally forgot to latch it. Eloise had left it invitingly open a few times herself, when her husband was at work, but the dog only sauntered away for a few hours and then returned to protect the house from children and blowing papers.

And, today, Herb had been the last member of the family in. Furious though he might be when he discovered the dog's disappearance, because it had become a kind of tug-of-war between them, he would be on shaky ground in blaming her.

Eloise turned back the coverlet on the nearest twin bed and stepped out of her shoes. Then, even though no sun was going to slant in from the dark west and dazzle her awake just as she was dropping off, she drew the front curtains.

Deborah Kingsley's body had been released to the funeral home early that morning. Hallam, expecting to find the house telephone covered by a relative or friend, felt it to be an omen of sorts when the brother answered instead. Remembering the boy's whiteness on their last encounter, he put no questions but said only that he would be there in fifteen minutes.

He knew better than to hope for a search warrant from the present magistrate at this stage. Gates, who owned a prospering meat market, also bred English bulldogs and was in demand as a judge at local shows. Even in the instance of a mixed breed, his sympathy would be automatically with McFee.

There had been the usual number of dogs in Hallam's child-hood, and the usual fondness; the bitterness to come would

*114*

have seemed impossible then. He was aware without having to think about it that a dog with the approximate bone structure of a German shepherd could survive, for a time at least, an accident that would have killed an Afghan hound.

Young Deborah Kingsley had managed to avoid hitting a dog on the afternoon before she died. She had seen and spoken to the man with it. Suppose someone else had not had a chance to react as quickly, struck the same dog glancingly, and lost control of the car with resulting injuries?

The Friday traffic sheets Hallam had requested showed a late-afternoon accident on Mission Road, two miles from the Kingsley house, with no other vehicle involved. A tow truck had been necessary for the front-damaged car and an ambulance for the woman driver, still in the hospital's intensive care unit. Her husband had been bewildered as well as shocked; his wife had a perfect thirty-year driving record.

Presumably, when questions were allowed, the woman would be able to describe what had happened. It was the kind of story that the *Pippin News* carried in detail, and to which Deborah, with her strong feelings in that area, would have responded with her own description.

Pippin had a leash law. On the surface, McFee in his small stark house was hardly a target for a wrongful-injury suit; but it was a first principle of police work that the surface was nothing to go by.

Kieran Kingsley, his stunned look replaced by a subdued excitement at being of special interest to a detective, let Hallam into a silent living room, which breathed recent death from its bare polished tables, immaculately plumped couch and chair cushions, pots of flowers ranged along mantelpiece and hearth. This was now only a place to receive callers.

Hallam's opening, "Ever seen this man before?" of the quick snapshot of McFee in his doorway that the photo lab had done their best with brought a studying, "No. Is he the guy who did it?"

"That's what we're trying to find out."

The boy led the way into the dining room with an air of new habit. Here the chairs around the table were at pulled-out angles, and two ashtrays, an open address book, and a box of stationery had been in use. There was neither sight nor sound of the old black and white spaniel who had had to be pushed away distractedly two nights ago because, muzzle on knee after knee, he kept demanding to know why everybody was up and dressed at that hour.

Hallam understood why. The spaniel had belonged to the dead girl, and just now its puzzled eyes could not be borne.

Hallam took out his cigarettes. "A dog ran in front of your sister's car on Friday afternoon. Did she say where that happened?"

"River Road, when she was about halfway home from the store." The boy narrowed his lashes in concentration. "The last she saw of the dog, it had run off behind a stone wall across the way."

"Did she describe the dog?"

"Only that it was funny-looking."

At some point Belinda Grace had said that McFee's dog, although reasonably accurate as to markings, looked like a German shepherd standing in a ditch.

"And the man—what about him?"

Kieran shook his dark head. "All Deb said was that she yelled at him and told him she worked at the emergency animal clinic and—get this—he called the dog a her when it was a male."

That stopped Hallam for seconds until he saw the intent. Narrow squeak, pour of adrenalin, relatively inexperienced driver too shaken to have noticed gender. Had the dog caused trouble in the same way before? Whatever the reason, the owner hadn't wanted the incident reported accurately.

The boy had to answer the telephone twice during the next ten minutes, his control threatened only when he gave his sister's present whereabouts as Fanshawe Mortuary. Hallam used the intervals to let his mind circle over River Road.

Old, settled, quiet, a preponderance of its properties handed down over generations, it was not a professional stamping ground. It made a pleasant drive in spring and summer, however, and he had traversed it often enough with Sue. The trouble was that low stone walls abounded.

Between telephone calls, Hallam learned that Deborah had not mentioned her fright to her parents—she knew that if she did, every future departure in her car would call forth an admonition to drive carefully—and that the Kingsley shopping was done at the Safeway.

"Halfway home" would give him an approximate area, but there must be a more time-saving method than that. Could he do what he had done with Belinda Grace?

He began to put questions to Kieran. Fifteen minutes later he drove up to a serene time-darkened house under trees, where the mailbox had a freshly hand-lettered "Callahan" over a painted-out but still legible "Ivy."

A machine-gun chatter of barks burst forth from within before there was a chance to use the well-polished brass knocker. It occurred to Hallam to hope unrealistically that when this case was over he would never see or hear another dog.

Hallam read the local paper from cover to cover every week, much as a stockbroker devoted himself to daily financial publications, and remembered that a Mrs. Ivy had died not long ago. He had never met her, but he had often, in the town, seen the smallish, brisk, gray-haired woman who opened the door; in fact, he had the distinct impression that she was or had been a nurse.

She was ringless, not much of a guide these days, but in view of her age Hallam tried a "Miss Callahan?" He introduced himself, complete with credentials, and told her why he was there: a near accident because of a loose dog here, a suspicious accident with serious injury less than a mile away and within the same time frame, a possible connection between the two.

"I don't think I can help you, but come in," said Miss

Callahan. Although the long, fringy dog was now sitting with an air of duty accomplished, she said sharply, "Roger, go to your bed."

To Hallam's surprise, the dog trotted obediently to a basket in the corner and settled on its haunches, eyes sparkling with interest under fronds of hair.

"It can't possibly have been my dog. He has an enclosed run in the back and he is never loose," said Miss Callahan. She bent to pick up a dead leaf that had drifted in with Hallam's entry; when she straightened, the effort had left her face oddly suffused. "Late Friday afternoon, did you say?"

Hallam nodded.

"I wasn't home. I help out at the blood-pressure clinic every Friday, and I didn't get home until after dark, so I'm afraid I'm of no use to you."

From her extremely high color, Hallam wondered how often Miss Callahan had her own blood-pressure checked. "That's too bad. According to a witness, the dog's owner, or at least the man with it, was in your driveway. Does he," he took out the snapshot of McFee again, "look at all familiar?"

Miss Callahan accepted it with steady fingers, examined the slightly blurred features far more rapidly than Kieran Kingsley had, and handed it back. "No."

Behind her, the dog stepped out of his basket and hurried from the room as if to answer a telephone ringing in a register undetectable by human ears. Within a matter of seconds there was a very different and actual sound, a series of subterranean efforts with which Hallam was all too familiar.

Roger, if that was his name, was being extremely sick.

# Chapter
# Fourteen

Hattie got rid of the detective with the authoritative speed she had used so often to eject visitors when a patient was visibly tiring. While the front door was closing behind him she was out at the back, setting Roger down on the grass, watching him with frightened eyes.

It was the first time she had known him to vomit. His dinner had been the same as always, and he was a considered rather than a wolfish eater, sometimes coming cordially to see Hattie midway as if to inform her that the food was going down nicely. Sauteed mushrooms on toast not being to his taste, he hadn't even had a morsel of her lunch.

Now, enthralled at the manner of his exit because he enjoyed his rare carryings, he gazed up at Hattie, tail wagging in inquiry as to what should be their next joint venture. Receiving no clue, he trotted off to nose around his escape route at the corner of the run, his immediate goal ever since the event. Could it have been only the day before last?

At once, all Hattie's fears about the whole episode came

rushing back. When she had brought Roger inside, because he was clearly going to do nothing but potter and the dining room rug awaited, she poured herself a small, uncharacteristic brandy.

There was no doubt in her mind that Roger was the dog for whom the police lieutenant was searching. Her denial of it, a contradiction of a basic honesty, had made her go as hot as fire, but what was she to do when she saw her entire future beginning a perilous topple?

Serious injury, he had said. If she were sued for what could be a staggering sum, would the trust pay? And if it did, how would she be looked upon as guardian?

The mention of a man in her driveway had given her a moment of real dread, and she had only glanced at the photograph to see, under the circumstances, who it was not. He was coincidental, she had said to herself with a relief of which she did not want to know the exact components; in pursuit of directions or—the afternoon had been windy—simply out for a walk, stepping into the shelter of the lilacs to light a cigarette or a pipe.

She cleaned the rug, an older and thinner Persian than the one in the living room, with flowers and vines of cream and turquoise and peach and coral woven into its very deep blue. Roger sat down attentively beside her. The cat, on a chair with paws folded under, watched the proceedings with an air of virtuous disgust.

What had made Roger throw up with such violence? Some dreadful trophy like a poisoned rat or mouse brought back from his illicit roaming and then cached? But poison did not lie in the system like a time bomb, and he had been perfectly all right when she left the house.

Hattie had once worked for an allergist, and recalled his painstaking reconstruction of a patient's day when there had been an unusual, unheralded attack of asthma. She went back over her own.

*     *     *

She had been later than she expected in getting home, and not only because of waiting for the hail to stop. The locksmith, with whom she was on gossiping terms because she had nursed his wife through a mastectomy, had kept her before that with an exciting bit of news that had not yet gotten into print. Benjamin Wells knew everything before it got into print.

Did Hattie know the Van Pattens? She did, by hearsay, along with the rest of the town. They had moved to Pippin about a year ago, a mid-thirtyish couple who promptly proceeded to dazzle.

No one was quite sure what Van Patten did—"consultant" was bandied about—but they bought a house that could not have cost less than two hundred thousand dollars, joined the yacht club, and drove about in matching steel-blue Cadillacs. Their entertaining provided the *Pippin News* with columns of type.

"Declaring bankruptcy," said Benjamin Wells trenchantly. "Makes you think, don't it?"

It didn't make Hattie think. For all of her working life she had put a punctilious percentage of every paycheck into her savings account, bought sheets and towels only at white sales, watched until there was a special on bacon. To her, living up to or well beyond one's income in order to lure moneyed flies into the web was as unimaginable as existence on a belly-dancing circuit.

She had fed Roger upon her return to the house, had her lunch, discovered when she took him outside as requested, without his leash because the side gate to the front lawn was closed and he was safe under her eye, the trash can blown over by the morning's winds. Like all dogs, Roger regarded this as a cornucopia, and romped off with what she found presently to be his old and linty chew stick, discarded there the evening before along with the remains of his rubber frog.

Hattie had taken it away from him out of principle, sealing it firmly into an empty soy sauce bottle. Could it, she wondered now, have spoiled? Her knowledge in this realm did not extend

*121*

beyond catnip mice, but it stood to reason that in order to appeal over shoes or gloves or chair legs the sticks were dipped in or impregnated with some substance.

To be on the safe side, she disposed of the rest of the box. With her calm restored, or so she thought, she went upstairs and brought down her suit jacket for the administering of the pastel chalk suggested by the girl who had been such a pleasant fringe benefit to waiting out the weather.

She had to turn on lights for the process, and when she had finished making a thick, powdery blend of green and white and a touch of black on a paper towel and stroked it into the knitted fabric it was time to draw the curtains. The night shut snugly out, she held the jacket at arm's length and surveyed it, pretending that she was one of the Aintrees.

Perfect, unless you knew exactly where to look. In a few minutes she would get dressed, because the drive to the Farrises' took almost fifteen minutes. There had been no opportunity to buy wine as her contribution to the evening, but in the cabinet under the stove there was an unopened bottle of—

Although to Hattie the night was soundless, Roger flashed out of his basket with a bark so sudden and shattering that it produced an unpleasant sensation in her chest.

She threw her jacket at a chair, snatched him up as he began further barking, ran with him to the kitchen, stood around a corner with her heart pounding and her calm shivered into a crazy pattern. There had been no thought at all involved. A car door slammed and the door knocker fell, but as long as she held him cradled against her like a long hairy infant Roger would be silent.

He rolled his eyes imploringly at her, and Hattie gave him exactly the little jiggles she would have given a baby about to make trouble. The knocker sounded again, and long seconds of silence—*who was out there?*—were followed by the echoes of retreat.

Donald, Hattie found, leaving her sanctuary and twitching

cautiously at a fold of curtains. Presumably she would be seeing him at dinner and if he had had thoughts of picking her up he would have offered that by telephone. Her pulse was still speeding, but her fright now was at herself. What had happened to her, in a space of hours, that an approach after dark had seemed to convey a very real warning?

Roger, put down, uttered a few thwarted grunts without troubling to open his mouth. At some point, poison, the word in its cold surround of skulls and crossbones, had whirled through Hattie's brain, but as she collected her jacket and started up the stairs she assured herself that no one would dare. The investigation promised under the terms of Charlotte's will was a built-in safeguard.

In the reminding, she forgot, or because she was sixty-two and had just been terrified and Charlotte had after all died of a heart attack some defense mechanism did the forgetting for her, the other side of that coin. An investigation would show that Roger had indeed dug out of his run, the scratching of his furious forefeet erasing any indication of a preliminary helping hand, a morsel so enticing as to be nosed about in retrospect long afterward.

The lights of Donald's car had played along the low stone wall across the road as he left. The blackness behind the wall remained inviolate.

The baby's fretful crying woke Eloise Ripley to darkness and, after a few seconds of reorientation, something that frightened her badly. Nothing from below. The television set, reliable cover and distraction for the arrival of Brownie's purchaser, had been turned off.

How long had she slept; what time was it? On the bedside clock, five twenty-two. Eloise shot off the bed, slid into her shoes, and opened the door of the baby's room, pausing just long enough to snap on the light. The baby, so familiar with being sponged off like a kitchen counter after its meals, had yet to learn that this sign was not necessarily followed at once by a fresh diaper or whatever else it deemed necessary, and, staggerily upright in its crib, stopped crying at once.

Eloise ran down the stairs, still blinking a little at the lamps. It couldn't have been dark for more than a few minutes on even this overcast day. Had the telephone caller come and gone in the dusk; was the money already tucked under the swan?

No. Outside, Brownie went into a flurry of faithful barks.

In the living room, the embodiment of discontent, Herb sat in the reclining chair that his parents had tendered at Christmas. Eloise, throat beating with alarm, said brightly, "My, I had a long sleep. Not watching '60 Minutes'?"

"It's a repeat. They have a hell of a nerve," said Herb, black.

When you had been married to a man of infinite sameness for eight years, it wasn't hard to analyze this mood. His team had lost; he had thoughtlessly drunk up all the existing beer on their way to defeat; in order to acquire anymore on Sunday he would have to humble himself and borrow some from Keith Haslip, two houses down, with whom he had had such a severe falling out that they had divided a black eye and a split lip between them.

And if he went outside now there was a very good chance that he would encounter . . .

Discovery was not even to be thought about in his present mood. As if he had stared directly into her brain, Herb said with the restlessness of a man looking for something to criticize, "You feed Brownie today?"

It couldn't be a trap; the dog was still demonstrably there. Eloise said, "No, I've been saving him some—"

"Bert, get up and go feed Brownie." Herb turned perversely on his son, on the floor poring over a comic book. "Your mother isn't supposed to do everything around here."

"He can't; I have to take the gristle off the bones." Even to desperate Eloise it sounded like gibberish, but the child could not be allowed to leave the house either. God above, was that the soft and nearing sound of a car engine?

Rapidly, she turned on the television set with a clicking change of channels. "I'll do it right now. Shall I get you a beer while I'm at it?"

"We're all out."

"Oh, are we really?" Arch, with a great effort, because even over the noise of a game show she could hear Brownie falling silent in mid-bark. "Tell you what, if you change Dawnelle I might just have a little surprise for you when you come down."

Eloise had learned long ago to keep a small reserve in the garage for whatever domestic crisis might arise. When Herb had gone willingly upstairs, she sped to the kitchen and made a loud business of filling a bowl with dry dog food. Then she opened the back door and walked outside.

Straining, she heard not a single footstep. From half a block away, a car engine came quietly to life.

The single window in the baby's room looked down at the rear. Eloise decanted the dog food into the feeding dish and slipped around the corner of the house, calling echoingly, "Brownie? Here, Brownie!" as a pair of taillights winked out of sight.

In spite of being coatless, she didn't feel the cold. She headed unerringly for the plastic swan although she had turned off the bedroom light and that side of the front lawn was in darkness.

Under the swan was the soft, heavy, almost oily fold of bills. Eloise whipped them into the pocket of her skirt, changed her mind, flattened them out, inserted them into the lining of one shoe. Then she ran for the garage.

She was none too early getting back inside with her three cans of beer. Herb, entering the kitchen with the now dry and calm baby, said as she had expected him to, "You get Brownie?"

"No, the gate was open—don't look at me—and he must have gone chasing after something, but he'll come back."

Eloise gazed clear-eyed at her husband, wriggling the toes of her right foot luxuriously. "He always does. You want to wait a while or should I turn on the oven for the pizza?"

On Westmorland Drive, the braver of McFee's few neighbors had turned out on this bitter evening to watch the police activity, most of it concentrated behind the house under a glaring white light rigged into place.

He had not been popular in his six months' tenure, even though people on this grim road tended to keep to themselves, and an aged woman in black said with an air of pronouncement, "The wicked flee where no man pursueth."

"They also duck child-support payments," said the girl next to her. With her square bangs and square jaw and straight, tight clasp of gold hair, she might have been a court figure in a Gobelin tapestry. She was a Ms. of some firmness, and had two children of preschool age. "I read an article about that last week, and the country is full of them."

Hallam, behind the house watching the opening of an impromptu grave, did not hear this observation, but would in any case have brushed it away as if to avoid any blurring of the clear, concise drawing in his mind.

McFee's flight had been planned in advance. The wiping out of any smallest personal clue could not have been managed in the time involved, even by a man living alone. There was no great effort involved in sweeping garments off hangers or emptying bureau drawers, but the stripping of shelves and medicine cabinet and the disposal of all correspondence, all papers of any kind, was something else.

Two empty wastebaskets, ash in the incinerator, a sparse collection of cans and bottles in the trash can outside the back door. The man had been erasing himself little by little.

Since shortly after midnight on Friday? But Hallam did not put a question mark after that.

The house had spoken of emptiness when he proceeded there after his abruptly terminated interview with Miss Callahan, and his judicious manipulation of the rickety back door in its warped frame had confirmed the fact.

"I thought I heard someone groaning inside," he had said, explaining the situation to the magistrate, Gates. "Must have been the wind over the marsh." And, to bolster his urgent request for a search warrant, "There's been some very recent digging in the back yard. I think it's of the essence to have a look at that."

Gates, caught during the closing minutes of a football game, had said yes, all right, go ahead—and now the flare of light was picking up something alien to the dark crumbles of earth being whisked aside with care after the first brisk shoveling.

Not surprisingly, a tuft of animal hair, the light brown ends glinting in this radiance. No dog, but Hallam could guess where it reposed now. How many acres of marsh out there?

In his first frustration at finding a vacated shell he had tried to visit the blame on Belinda Grace and her kind mention of a dog hair on the slacks that hadn't been brushed against by a dog. That little detail had bitten a good forty minutes out of the afternoon.

But would he have followed her home if she had been a dumpy uninteresting fifty instead of bemusing in her slender-waisted coat and her hat? Wouldn't he, failing Sergeant Uffi, have commandeered a patrolman to pick up the hair for comparison?

He had pursued instead a line of inquiry that bordered on the personal. He had seen her before only in a housecoat or her brisk clinic garb, and for the first time, although perversely determined not to let her see it, he had had an inkling of what Norman Comstock had done to her.

He owed her an apology of sorts, because there had been a reply from Bell Falls, Pennsylvania.

# Chapter
# Fifteen

"His name is Jamie. Isn't he a sweetums?" said the new girl at the clinic when she handed over to Belinda at four o'clock. She was about nineteen and arrestingly fat. "I could just eat him up."

Unhappy phrasing, thought Belinda, but the Maltese terrier, a small explosion of fluffy white fur, was indeed a beguiling creature. Apart from the occasional tilt of his head and the cast on one rear leg, he might have been a stuffed toy, a decoy for trembling animals encountering strange hands and alien smells for the first time.

He was also, demonstrably, a patient of note. A metal panel that made two smaller cages out of a large one had been removed, and he perched on a cushion instead of a section of blanket or toweling. A few toys had been brought with him, and when the girl—Joy, Belinda remembered now—said cajolingly, "Where's your stocking, Jamie?" he hobbled off his cushion and picked up a red felt Christmas arrangement with a gilt J, tucking it into what looked like a little black smile.

"He was a good boy, yes he was!" cried Joy, who even on brief acquaintance was distressingly coy. "His owner is picking him up at around five. Kitty there," she nodded at the cage above the terrier's, where a Persian cat was haughty even in unconsciousness, "had an exploratory at three, but we're doing very well."

Could she be an out-of-work nurse? Impossible; hospitals snapped them up as soon as they became available. Patients could be and frequently were made much of by the staff, but a frown clouded Dr. Kitsch's brow at any approach to bedside manner. He had once, overhearing a client being assured over the telephone that "we ate our breakfast," said augustly, "We may lose ours" as he passed by.

Belinda's brain reported all this to her with the accuracy of total uninvolvement. Was it the effect of the whole strange day with its bombardment of personalities, or could it be narrowed down to lunch and the sensation of being whole again?

The clinic was exceptionally quiet when Joy had left. In contrast to the usual Sunday bustle, nobody waited in the reception area; the back ward was tenanted only by the cats and a Newfoundland who whined from time to time from sheer loneliness; there wasn't even any restocking to be done from the previous shift.

The situation explained itself when Dr. Cooper's door opened briefly on the sound of a transistor radio: "—and it's out of bounds on the Dallas forty-five. Third and ten, and Denver wants a time out . . ."

Everybody would come at once after the game, thought Belinda, and Dr. Cooper would grow tense and snappish because Dr. Kitsch was on backup and that summons would be put off as long as possible. Her foreboding was detached; in her present strange state, half of being immersed in another world, half of balancing along the top of a wall, she felt quite able for Dr. Cooper.

She went to check on the Newfoundland and say hello to the donor cats. The one who had been called into service for the Persian's surgery regarded her with distant calm; the other, marmalade-barred yellow, poked out a curved paw, claws sheathed, in greeting.

Hattie Callahan's guardianship, about which Donald had told her briefly, wasn't really singular; people must make similar arrangements for their pets far more often than appeared in the newspapers. In the case of mynahs it must make the relatives really sit up and take umbrage. Wasn't that life span close to a parrot's?

Donald clearly didn't resent his aunt's will. Even though he was at the beck and call of the residents at the Steptoe house with a new book under way, he had had an air of wry admiration. Why the forehead-pinching doubt, then, the something like guilt?

When the telephone rang, Belinda answered it with the speed of someone watching over a sleeping household. A woman with an extraordinarily low-pitched voice said that she was new in town, had been referred by a long-time client of Dr. O'Neill's, and needed to know how much tranquilizer it was safe to give her ten-pound dog before an imminent flight.

"He's a barker, very high-strung, and as he'll be in an onplane carrier . . ."

Belinda transferred the call to Dr. Cooper. As if only a single ring had been needed to unstop the dike, a man telephoned at once about his spider monkey, the tip of whose tail had been bitten off by the family dog in an excess of high spirits; could he bring it in right away? While Belinda was saying yes and had the monkey been in before, the buzzer sounded and a man arrived with a limping blue merle collie. Sunday was starting a return to normal.

Alone among the vets, Dr. Cooper regarded the attendants as necessary beasts of burden, reasonably faithful but stupid, and when he was working he was at no particular pains to conceal his view. He had taken a blood sample from a lop-eared puppy, and Belinda had put it in the centrifuge, when the phone rang.

She answered, listened, said, "I don't know. Just a second," and covered the mouthpiece. "Do we board dogs?"

Dr. Cooper finished smoothing tape over the puppy's foreleg and turned elaborately, without hurry. "You do know the meaning of the word emergency, Miss—?"

Like the others, he had always called her by her first name; he was doing this to put on a fine edge for the benefit of the dog's owner, who turned away in surprise and embarrassment.

"Grace. I'll look it up in my *Webster's* unabridged when I get home," said Belinda, made reckless by her day, "but I *think* it has something to do with situations that call for immediate action."

The peaked eyebrows climbed toward the clustering curls, as marvelingly displeased as if his burro had suddenly started to tell him boring anecdotes. It occurred to Belinda that it would be an enormous satisfaction to steal into his house and smuggle a powerful depilatory into his shampoo.

"And what emergency have we here?" inquired Cooper. "A fire? A flood?"

Over half the cages in the big room were empty. Belinda uncovered the mouthpiece and said levelly to the woman whose voice had sounded familiar, "I'm sorry, I'm told we don't."

She knew the time of that call because she had checked the wall clock for the centrifuging, which took five minutes. It was five minutes of six.

Jamie's owner arrived, a tall rosy-cheeked girl in velvet-collared tweed, and Belinda handed over a sheet of instructions, which included the necessity for a plastic bag over the cast every time he went outside. The terrier stumped bravely as far as the door, sounding more like a pirate than thirteen pounds of snowy fluff, and left a few involuntary smiles in his wake.

It was well after six-thirty when a man called to ask in a brogue if his missing dog had by any chance ended up at the clinic. He couldn't just lay his hands on the license number, but it was a male and partly dachshund—"the long-haired kind, like"—and light brown with touches of dark gray around the face and haunches.

Belinda said they had no dog of that description and asked, before she remembered that on Sundays the number did not answer—there was an employee there to receive animals, but that was all—if he had tried the shelter. He said yes, and thanked her and hung up.

Perhaps he had accidentally killed the dog in his driveway and didn't want to admit it to a family member listening nearby? On the other hand, the clinic had the shelter's unlisted number in case they needed a donor dog, not kept on the premises because of the upkeep involved, and possibly by way of a former attendant the man with the brogue had it too.

When the spider monkey departed, jaunty in a tiny emerald wool dress and with a diminutive sock of bandaging on its tail, a few flakes of snow came spinning in to retract into points of moisture on the polished tile. Even though this featheriness bore no resemblance to hail, Belinda knew at once who had called with the inquiry that had touched off Dr. Cooper's temper.

Hattie Callahan. Was the engagement implied by the very light-eyed man in the watch cap for tonight? If so, she was reluctant to leave her valuable dog behind; she had wanted a night's harbor for it.

Belinda had been warned at the outset that the preservation of the high floor shine was something of an obsession with the director. She went rapidly back to the storage room for the spare strip of carpeting, this one handily mud-colored, to put down just inside the front door.

Impossible not to remember, because she was briefly alone out here thanks to the dinner hour or the starting snow, that Deb Kingsley had gone through exactly the same process a few minutes before she died.

With the dog cut off in mid-bark, thought Donald with a touch of grimness as he drove away, the message was unmistakable. Hattie was not receiving. Coupled with what Belinda had said was her unaccompanied state that afternoon, on the occasions he had seen her in the town since his aunt's death Roger had always been a front-seat passenger.

Could Cherry possibly be right?

He put himself back in the little front hall, picking up where she had broken off as Belinda appeared on the stairs. "If Hattie weren't such a pillar of rectitude, you would be tempted to think—what?"

"That maybe that dog only looks like Roger," said Cherry calmly, putting on the glove she had been slapping at the banister. "There was something odd about him yesterday— he didn't recognize me, for one thing—and there was something odd about her, too. When someone knocked at the door I'll swear she jumped, even though it turned out to be an electrician."

The idea was so flabbergasting that Donald could only stare. *Hattie?* Locating a stand-in for Roger, who had met with a fatal accident, so that she could continue to benefit under Charlotte Ivy's will? The French had a word for his condition: *bouleversée.* Here he had been, wondering who on his short list had flipped rapidly through his notebook in search of details of the dog's provenance . . .

Hattie had been at her house when he returned from his successful mission, explaining that if the dog was unacceptable for any reason the owner would like to be informed so that she could find him another home. He had either mentioned the name or written it down.

"It would be a temptation, wouldn't it?" said Cherry, opening the door. "I mean, here you are one minute, all nicely taken care of, and the next. . . . I haven't breathed a word of this to Laurence or Nan, in case I'm wrong." Cat's smile, warmly raspberry, and shining dark glance before she let herself out. "I thought you'd be the one."

Her idea had obviously been for him to drive to Hattie's right away. But Mrs. Calvacaressi's bathtub drain was stopped up again—from the frequency with which Donald had to remove stubborn mats of hair he wondered that she wasn't entirely bald—and Phineas Coe, catching him on the stairs in the act of visible superintending, hated to be a bother but his kitchen sink . . .

When he did force himself to go to Hattie's, her car wasn't there, and then had come his lunch with Belinda, his island of pure pleasure. By that time, checking up or hounding down had become an unpleasant, Monday kind of thing to do.

Belinda had said uncomplicatedly of Hattie, "She seems very nice," and it had struck him as both a reproach and a basic folly. Why hadn't any of them tried to know Hattie better? It was true that up until two years ago she had worked, and answered when asked idly why she never joined them for drinks at his aunt's that when she got home all she wanted to do was put her feet up, and it was also true that she had seemed to back away from her younger relatives.

Still. Hattie looked too forthright to be shy or uncertain, but who could tell? And Donald was indirectly responsible for Roger and the whole situation, which, examined now, had strong elements of worry.

He was home. So, from their lights, were Phineas Coe and Mrs. Calvacaressi; but for Donald the old house was empty with Belinda unobtainable at her job. What frightful hours, he thought with indignation.

Inside, he went straight to the directory and telephone and dialed J. S. Wishart for the third time in three days. Logic said that anyone in quest of a dog to pass off as Roger would have to go to the source, and there had been a littermate, also male and an apparent twin, in the carton on the old car's back seat.

The blankly ringing line said that, as before, Miss Wishart was not at home. Donald had to remind himself that unless they were expecting calls of paramount importance people did not stay by their telephones; they shopped, went to the post office, visited friends, dined out. Or when they were in residence they took showers.

In any case, wouldn't anyone carrying out a deception of major proportions pay well for silence?

Donald made himself a drink and paced about with it. Hattie could not hide behind drawn curtains forever, but even if he could identify the dog as a plant what would he do about it? He could use his share of the estate, God knew, and he suspected that, appearances to the contrary, Laurence and Nan would far prefer not to wait years for theirs either, but Hattie was sixty-odd. He could not see himself as the agent of her being stripped and disgraced.

On the other hand, the situation couldn't simply be left dangling. If the real Roger no longer existed, perhaps the three of them could make a private financial arrangement for Hattie—but would acquisitive Cherry go along with that? Would Peter Farris?

The Aintrees were firm nondroppersin on each other; they met by prearrangement every few weeks. Even if it had been otherwise, even if Laurence or Nan lived a five-minute drive away instead of at the other end of the long curving town, Donald had no intention of consulting them just yet.

Tomorrow, by hook or crook, he would see Hattie and have a look at the dog. What difference could a day make?

There was a timorous knock, recognizable, which would go right on tap-tapping until Donald did something about it. He snatched up the clear glasses, dark-rimmed, which had little effect on Mrs. Calvacaressi but had proved useful in the present case, and opened his door to Phineas Coe.

"I'm such a pest," said Coe accurately, "but I have just surprised an earwig in my bathroom, a large one, and where there is one earwig there must—"

"Good," said Donald, interrupting with force. "You didn't frighten it, I hope?"

Coe gaped at him.

"The earwig is the early scout for the very valuable ladybug," said Donald, adjusting his glasses halfway down his nose,

135

"and I'm sure I don't have to tell you about ladybugs."

"I never knew that," said Coe slowly. "An ecological thing. To think I came within a hair of—well, not stepping on it, but wrapping it in tissue and flushing it on its way."

"I'm glad you came to me," said Donald, benign, and closed the door.

It was too early for dinner after a late lunch. An endless stretch of time yawned between now and approximately twenty after twelve, when Belinda would come back. What to do with the cumbersome hours? He couldn't stay here; in spite of his temporary diversion he was making himself nervous.

He emptied his drink, broke a five-year rule, and went out to see a movie.

# Chapter
# Sixteen

"Hattie. *Here* you are, come in," said Nan, holding the front door wide. She was wearing something long and tangerine, bolder than her usual colors. "Don't worry about the snow, we've been listening to the forecast and they say flurries."

"And will keep on saying flurries until the drifts close over their heads," said Peter, winking at Hattie as he took her coat.

It was a pretty hall, or foyer, Hattie supposed, carpeted in deep blue, with a mirror to one side of the stairway's foot and on the other a cushioned white iron bench next to a marble-topped table, which held a foreign-looking telephone. She waited until she was clear of it and in the living room, where Laurence and Cherry were on their feet, before she delivered the utterance that had occurred to her as an aftermath of her strange fright while she hid in the kitchen from Donald.

"I'm afraid I'm late." She was, deliberately. "I had to drop Roger off at the emergency clinic."

The lie practiced in the car came out with ease, and four faces turned attentive. Nan, with an inviting gesture at one end of a couch, said with no traceable irony, "That's too bad. What's wrong?"

"Nothing, probably, but he didn't seem quite himself," said Hattie, sedate even now about mentioning physical symptoms at the cocktail hour, "and I thought it wouldn't hurt to have them take a look."

"There speaks the medical community," said Laurence with some dryness.

It was fair enough—there were doctors who thought nothing of saying that there would be no harm in a complete G.-I. series when the patient was simply complaining of a dry throat— but Hattie flushed. It was not a help when Cherry said, "Hattie, what a pretty suit," and then proceeded to stare fixedly at the front of it.

From somewhere there was a muffled barking: the German shepherd, incarcerated for the evening. Peter extended a glass to Hattie. "Nan tells me Irish whiskey for you. Better catch up with the rest of us; you look a bit fraught."

He continued down the room to the stereo. "Anyone who objects to Edith Piaf say *non*." He brought the intimate voice alive, turned it pleasantly low, and said to Nan, appearing with a plate of toasted cheese triangles for the coffee table, "I think I'll give Donald a ring, this is absentminded even for him."

Hattie had wondered about Donald's absence—"Just family," Nan had said in her invitation—but to ask might suggest discontent with the present company. Cherry said, "Talk about fraught. Laurence, tell Hattie about your terrible siege."

Laurence glanced at his wife with mild surprise but launched obediently into a list of aches, pains, and degrees of temperature. Edith Piaf was seductive in the background. Hattie, registering the urbanity with which Laurence's trials and tribulations were being absorbed by these handsome people, said meanly to herself: Can they be putting on all this sophistication just for me?

"No answer, and I let it ring for quite a while, so he must be on his way," said Peter, coming back; but he was frowning.

Nan, who had stopped smoking months ago, lit a cigarette. "You did tell him tonight?"

"No, I told him a year from St. Swithin's Day," said Peter, and then, "Of course I did. But I caught him at—it must have been ten-thirty or after, because you'd gone to bed, and sometimes he's a nonlistener. Well, let's not die of thirst while we wait."

If Hattie had been thoroughly at ease in these surroundings she might have noticed that a tension had come into the room, might even have been able to track it. As it was, she held out the glass she was surprised to find empty and said, "Could you make mine a little lighter this time?"

Donald wasn't coming; from his oddly timed arrival at her house she was suddenly sure of that, although there was no way to tell them. And what exactly had been the purpose of that visit? Was it conceivable that he had expected Roger to be sick, that he would have said something like, "My car's warm, why don't you let me take him to a vet for you?" and that somewhere along the way—?

In that case she would have planted her lie, the tale that embraced the fact of a strange man on her property, in precisely the wrong place.

"Everything all right, Hattie?" Peter, giving her a fresh drink, smiled at her with his eyebrows up.

"Yes, fine," said Hattie, because all at once it was. No one could get into the secure house without breaking a window or smashing a lock, and even if he planned to inflict mortal harm upon Roger, which she couldn't bring herself to believe, Donald was far too intelligent for that.

The talk turned to television commercials, and they vied with each other as to the greatest horrors. The German shepherd had subsided into an occasional throaty whine; as if reminded, Cherry sneezed fastidiously from time to time. Nan came and went, at one point producing more golden triangles, which Hattie looked at wistfully but did not dare touch because in her system toasted cheese turned into boiling oil.

Presently, a light clash of silver from the dining room partly visible through a wide arch indicated that a place setting was being removed: Donald had been given up on. When Nan announced that dinner would be in fifteen minutes, Peter said, "She means business. Last call," and began to collect empty glasses invitingly. Cherry and Nan declined; Hattie, sure of herself on the strength of the single whiskey that was her regular evening practice and consumed over a leisurely period of time, went along with Laurence and Peter.

How nice they suddenly all were, even Cherry, and how warm and friendly the room, which at first had seemed to contain a jarring amount of stone and glass. I have simply never given them a try before, thought Hattie, admiring her own balanced perception. I have judged a book by its cover. Their covers.

"Peter?" called Nan from a great distance away. "You can carve for me, please."

Except for a bowl of salad on the dining room table with its ice-blue candles, serving in the Farris house was done in the kitchen. Hattie, who had been very hungry half an hour earlier, found herself staring without much interest at sliced roast lamb and saffron rice. Along with a lack of mint sauce there was no sign of rolls or biscuits, which was no doubt how the Farrises stayed so lean and spruce.

But she must eat, and at once, however disinclined; she knew that. She tried the saffron rice first, because it did not require a knife, and it was so strong that she was driven to the wine glass, which she had sternly not raised or touched in response to Peter's hazily heard toast.

Still, across from her, Cherry was saying in a far echo much like Nan's, "This is divine," and an immaculate girl in a white wool dress of Chinese cut must know what she was talking about. Peter, on Hattie's left, had done some courteous helping of gravy and salad, but even when she had drawn some slow and measured deep breaths, which she thought went unobserved, Hattie regarded the salad as much too tricky and slippery.

Gravy did not make the lamb submissive to her fork, and the knife was impossible.

A dim recollection of her professional way with hospital patients who put the covers back on their plates after a single glance came back to Hattie: "You can't expect to get your strength back if you don't eat."

So, the rice, bitter though it was.

What happened to her happened with suddenness. Shaming voices, which she could not attach to faces, flipped past her like leaves in a high wind, to be folded forever into darkness:

"What's the matter with her?"

"She's had too much to drink. I *thought* that last one—"

"We could put her in the guest—"

"And have her wake up here? She'd never want to face any of us again."

"I agree. Home, right now, while she can still walk. You can walk, can't you, Hattie? Hattie?"

And that was it; that was all.

The dog in the furnace room had been awake for some time although he was still too groggy to take much interest in his surroundings. He could hear the presence of another dog not far away, but he knew from the deep chest sound that it was a bigger dog and he would not have barked back, in this strange place, even if his muzzle had not been tied.

Now, he made no objection when the beam of a flashlight found him and he was picked up and carried out into the cold.

Belinda's temper, increasingly tried by Dr. Cooper, remained under control until after eight o'clock.

Although the circumstances warranted it, he did not have her call Dr. Kitsch and Hilda as backup. Instead, he gave her conflicting orders, snapped at her when she asked which he meant, seemed genuinely pleased at her difficulties with a catheter, stood with his arms folded dangerously when the telephone rang and it was Donald.

"Belinda. I'm sorry to bother you there and it's probably foolish to ask, but when you talked to Hattie this afternoon did she say anything about going somewhere tonight?"

The cocker spaniel on the table was ready for caging. Dr. Cooper left it there and listened openly. Belinda eyed him over the receiver and said, "Not directly, but she had to get a suit in condition for this evening and a man she knew stopped to talk to her and said something like, 'Don't forget.' "

Briefly, she described the watch cap, the extremely light gray eyes, the cleft chin. She added, "Oh, and she called a couple of hours ago to ask if we board dogs."

A short silence from Donald but not from the background; there were either a great many people in his apartment or he was calling from elsewhere. He said, "And do you?"

"No."

"Will you come in for a drink and some sustenance when you get home?"

"Yes."

"You're being eavesdropped on. I'll see you later."

"You seem to be losing the meaning of the word *emergency* again," said Dr. Cooper balefully when the receiver went down. "This is neither the time nor the place for personal calls."

Belinda could not know that one of his perfectly sound-looking white front teeth was being hammered with every beat of his heart, that antibiotics had not yet taken effect, that, on duty, he could not saturate himself with pain-killers.

She said composedly, "That happened to concern a client," because certainly Hattie Callahan must be somebody's client, and put the spaniel in a cage.

After that there was a brief halt in arrivals although the telephone sprang into action. Belinda relegated most of the calls to Dr. Cooper in his lair, took out the cards on animals to be brought in, checked the ones in tenancy. Through her fatigue she had a brink-edge happiness, which she did not look at too hard for fear of frightening it away, or construing it as the rarest of butterflies when it was only a destructive moth.

For all his needling, she was completely unprepared for the descent of Dr. Cooper, his lab coat not quite flying.

"Would you care to tell me," he said with ominous humility, "so that I can tell the director, to whom I am responsible, why the other employees have been asked to say if inquired of that you do not work here?"

Belinda's midsection went into an instant seethe of astonishment and then anger. "No, I would not. It's an entirely personal matter and has nothing to do with my job."

"I think that what amounts to dissimulation on the part of an employee is very much the business of the people who own and operate this clinic," said Dr. Cooper. His cheekbones burned. "Especially under the circumstances. And previous circumstances."

His tone might have been used to address a migrant worker in the habit of showing up drunk, and Belinda suddenly could not stand another minute of him. She walked out of the room, snapped on the light in the receptionist's office, pulled out the sliding board in the desk with its pasted-on list of names and telephone numbers.

She dialed. She said, "Hilda? Belinda. Things are desperate here, can you come in right away? Oh, good. Thanks."

Dr. Cooper, in the doorway, took an incredulous step forward. "It is not your decision to—"

"It is my decision to be out of here in ten minutes," said Belinda, crisp with rage, "and if anybody cares to send me a bill for Hilda's overtime I will send it right back. What you have been engaging in for the past two hours is harassment, pure and simple."

She left the office by its other door and went rapidly in the direction of the lockers, body humming with reaction, aware and not caring that this behavior could be called irresponsible. Overwork was bearable, but a vendetta in the course of it was something else again.

It was no real trouble to figure out who had given Dr. Cooper his information. Helpful Mrs. Espinosa, telling the new girl who her relief would be, and adding, "But if a man asks for her she'd rather he didn't know she works here." What better way for a new girl to prove her worth and loyalty to the clinic than by passing along inside information? Joy's was the only relevant voice that could have slipped by unrecognized in that flurry of calls.

Hilda lived only a few blocks away and had such tenure that she used her own key to let herself in at the back just two minutes after Belinda's hoped-for ten. She welcomed the over-time, but was puzzled by the apparent tranquility. "Where is everybody?"

"The rush died down a little while ago, but something's come up and I have to leave," said Belinda, not wanting to involve the other girl in any controversy. "I should warn you that Dr. Cooper is in a vile mood."

"He won't step on my little black toes," said Hilda, giving her a glance of amusement. Her tone changed as she watched Belinda buttoning her coat. "Are you okay?"

"Just," said Belinda, and managed a smile with difficulty; there were people who throve on scenes, but she wasn't one of them. She extricated her car keys. "Good-night, and good luck."

The snow had stopped. The shadows that Deborah Kingsley had dreaded lay on whiteness, virgin from this view except for the tracks made by Hilda's arrival, and the three vehicles there, iced on top, lightly furred on the sides.

Not three; four. There was a front bumper fractionally visible beyond Dr. Cooper's pickup with its camper shell.

By daylight it would have declared itself to be a car with engine trouble or a flat tire, left behind by a member of the cleaning crew. Now, with Hilda undoubtedly deep in the heart of the clinic and the door locked behind Belinda, a quality of cunning leaped into the night, woven skillfully into the slight shift of black branch outlines on snow.

"If you wait long enough and don't make a sound," William Grace had said immeasurable years ago to a child fretful with measles, "something is bound to come out."

And something had: a rabbit, hopping into a patch of cold moonlight, finding it suspect at once, freezing to an electric stillness.

Belinda broke out of her stillness and ran for her car.

The miraculous happened, the opposite of what her blood was sending her in drumming shorthand. The door key went in with accuracy, the engine caught on the first try, nothing came exploding into the flare of the headlights. She switched on her wipers to clear the windshield, backed in a wide, fast arc and followed Hilda's tire tracks to the nearer of the two exits.

The little interlude before she could slide into the traffic ought to have been calming—message mistaken, locked and perfectly functioning car poised in a bath of overhead light. Instead, her nerves paid her back for that confrontation in the surgery, and the hands that could not be busy with the steering wheel or the gearshift began an incipient shake.

Here was an opening, a refuge, and she ducked into it: home, hot bath, one of the tranquilizers she took perhaps four times a year. Time to look at what she had done to the immediate future, although she didn't regret it; if anything, she found in it a tiny core of returning self.

—And right behind her, face showing pale in the last streetlight before the road forked off into darkness because he was leaning well forward, wanting her to know who was going to do what he had in mind—Norman.

It was like a terrible revelation by lightning: the firmly cut lips compressed, the brows drawn with purpose. The avenging presence, which was not in Bennington, as Hallam had lightly suggested, but here, and on the hunt.

Belinda had let him do the driving on that one trip to her parents' house, because he had said that the carbon needed to be burned out of wherever carbon accumulated, and he was— a sometime auto mechanic—an expert, dazzling with the clutch, judging the exact half-second to whip out of a curve.

She was a capable driver, but Norman could run her off the road with ease, leaving her stunned and injured in a damaged car. He knew where she lived, so she couldn't bolt for there—but what about the first lighted driveway, hand on the horn as she approached?

Instinct, or some detail of which she had not taken real note in her overwhelming relief, made her test the horn. Nothing—but don't cry; that would only hasten disaster.

Not Joy who had fed Dr. Cooper that ammunition, but someone casually commandeered by Norman, who must have made at least one abortive attempt before he reached her at the clinic. How easily he could do it: a drink or two in a bar with a friendly female, a tale of having lost his job unjustly because of a woman named Grace who was there herself under false pretenses.

"What a shame. Why don't you blow the whistle on her?"

"I can't. She answers the phone, and she'd know my voice and hang right up."

"Well, she wouldn't know *my* voice. What's the number?"

Wasn't there a corner coming up, just beyond the huge old oak that had some historical significance? Could Norman be aware of it? Belinda gave the wheel a last-minute wrench, careened to her left, switched off her lights after a memorizing look.

He would have been on her at once if it hadn't been for a long furious blare of horn and the complaint of brakes. She made a right turn with only the snow to guide her and switched on her lights again, angling north and west, away from the Steptoe house, in search of a street with concealing traffic.

What she found had sudden familiarity: the distant shape of a severely steepled white church. She had been in this area on Zari's single guided tour; she had been here only this afternoon when Donald drove her home from lunch the long way. Had he turned to the right or left at the church before coming to a graceful old house of which he said, "That's Hattie's"?

The mirror showed a car emerging from a side road behind

her and accelerating with speed and purpose. The pressure in Belinda's throat built to the aching point. She couldn't drive through the night indefinitely; she had neither the gasoline nor the nervous reserve.

Here was the stop sign, and some oncoming traffic. She took a reckless gauge of it and shot across, cutting her lights for the second time, bumping along a spruce-bordered lane whose outline she remembered from the drive with Zari.

"Famous old cemetery, for us locals anyway. Sometime when you're feeling less cheerful you ought to come and read some of the epitaphs."

Epitaphs.

The light snow was being nibbled at by ground moisture, but there was still enough to show her a sharp corner. Branches swept the side of the car as she nosed around it, braked, turned the ignition key, and sat listening to her heart pounding the seconds away.

# Chapter
# Seventeen

". . . coffee, Hattie. You'll be fine, you've been walking and walking, but you must drink coffee."

Walking? It was lost in the blurred buzz of Hattie's brain. She was in her own bed, nightgowned, not even wondering how this had come about but aware remotely that she had been in a crisis of some kind. Obediently, because someone was seeing her through it, she drank a warm liquid held to her lips and sank back on her pillow.

"That's it. Now you can sleep."

Walking, coffee, and sleep bore no trace of paradox; Hattie had been offered a reward and she accepted it gratefully. The bedside lamp winked out on a glass from the bathroom, its residue clear, and a small memo pad, ballpoint pen beside it, which carried an underlined "Call Bernard Odom" in her handwriting.

The telephone on the night table's shelf had been pushed to the back. A trailing, groping hand would not be able to reach it.

Downstairs, there was no need for the kitchen light to be

flicked on. The brandy bottle was already on the counter, a pure gift like the memo pad, and the bottle of Irish whiskey had been lifted up carefully to join it. Used glass in the sink. A portion of lamb and innocent saffron rice, decanted from a plastic bag and indicating a scarcely touched dinner, reposed on one of Hattie's plates in the refrigerator.

Out through the back door, avoiding any contact with the bemused and submissive dog in the living room who might have passed for Roger except to the vet responsible for the neutering and the thorough physical examination the day after Charlotte's will had been read.

Good-night, Hattie.

No; good-bye, Hattie.

In his small office, Hallam did not immediately take his hand away from the receiver he had just put back in its cradle. The collapse of his case against McFee had sent up a cloud of bitter ash, and for the next ten or fifteen minutes at least there wasn't anything to be done about it.

McFee had certainly decamped in a hurry, but his dog, the keystone of the solid-seeming arch, was not a keystone after all. A half hour earlier, Uffi had been allowed to put a brief question to the woman injured in a one-car accident such an interesting distance from the scene of Deborah Kingsley's berating.

The woman was out of intensive care, bandaged but completely lucid. She had swerved to avoid a tiny black dog and had to swerve again for the young child pursuing it headlong. She had lost control as a result and met a hickory tree with force.

For good measure, she had never set eyes on McFee before.

His neighbors on Westmorland Drive were reluctant to talk about McFee, as if he might come storming back in retribution. A crone in black had volunteered that the wicked would flourish like the green bay tree, but Hallam already knew that. A chunky girl was of the opinion that he had a grudge against women in general.

He had been living in the rented house for about six months, keeping largely to himself and apparently with no job. There was no way of knowing where he came from as his car had carried a temporary license when he arrived.

It was at the very last house that Hallam saw the first deep flaw in his structure. Flight meant fear, but of what? An elderly retired couple who looked as dull and gray as a pair of beards but had the surprising habit of spending most of their evenings in the nearest tavern produced an answer.

Encountering McFee one evening, they had bought him a drink—for the first and last time, they said with emphasis. The television set was on, and before the bartender hastily switched channels a special about battered wives flashed on the screen. McFee had slapped his drink down on the table, said loudly, "Some of them ask for it," and walked out without another word.

"*And* he'd been married, and for quite a long time," said the gray wife significantly. "You could see the dent on his wedding finger. I said to Andrew right then and there, 'What do you want to bet that he knows a thing or two about battering?' What's more, he's never spoken to us since, has he, Andrew?"

Hiding from a charge of assault and battery? It would explain the ugly temper, the seclusion, the swift clean sweep; a man with a warrant out for him was apt to keep in a state of readiness. Learning late about the murder at the clinic, because he had no intimates, he had taken to his heels. It had the dismaying ring of truth even before Uffi's call from the hospital.

Hallam glanced at his watch, pulled the telephone closer, and dialed. Belinda Grace's number rang blankly, although she had now had a little over twenty minutes to reach home.

Something had come up, another attendant had told him when he called the clinic just too late. To Hallam, remembering Belinda as he had last seen her, that suggested a change from her working clothes and perhaps a bag to pack.

She wouldn't, would she, with her obvious fear of him, have been decoyed into meeting Norman Comstock somewhere?

In his single-minded pursuit of McFee—undoubted killer of

his dog, which wasn't even a misdemeanor—Hallam realized now that he had dismissed Norman Comstock much too lightly. He didn't like what he had heard from the Bell Falls police.

Comstock had come to their attention a year ago, when they had been summoned to the house of an osteopath, a Dr. Merriam, to evict by force a roomer who refused to leave. They did not arrive soon enough to suit the doctor, who filled the interval by throwing Comstock down the stairs. Comstock promptly filed charges, insisting that he had not been asked repeatedly to leave by Mrs. Merriam as alleged.

Comstock was thirty-two, the doctor's wife a motherly fifty-seven. Merriam, evidently realizing that the publicity would be damaging, settled privately with his ex-roomer and the charge was dropped. A discreet month later, the house burned to the ground. Arson was suspected, but Comstock had disappeared.

Between the lines, and according to the doctor's testimony, it was a chilling little tale. He and his wife had both taken to the young man and agreed to rent him a room because they had more than enough space, their grown children having departed. He was quiet and courteous—and he attached himself like a limpet. The household became a weird ménage à trois, with nothing sexual involved. Adjured to go, Comstock mowed the lawn instead, or tinkered successfully with Merriam's car. They had no privacy. It became unbearable.

Before being tried to the limit, Merriam dredged around among assorted colleagues and discovered that Comstock had months before broken off a course of psychiatric counseling. The counseling wasn't voluntary; it had been imposed as a condition of probation by a judge in a neighboring town. The root of Comstock's trouble seemed to be that he had been a foundling.

And was now a man to whom, once he had sought out and established a relationship, no woman could say a one-sided farewell without paying a forfeit.

Belinda Grace had paid hers, but then she had hung up on

Comstock when he telephoned her at the clinic. If he had not left Boston for Vermont as advertised, would he try to collect a second penalty?

Hallam found a Boston directory and dialed Belinda's apartment there. He got a strange female voice, which said surprisedly to his question that yes, she was Zari Zulalian, and no, she hadn't talked to Belinda that day. Was something the matter?

Hallam said untruthfully that he didn't think so—what point in alarming her, miles away?—but gave her his home telephone; he would appreciate her letting him know if she heard from Belinda.

He tried the Steptoe house again without success, sat staring at his desk for a minute or two, darkened his office, spoke briefly to the duty sergeant, and went out to his car.

"Hattie?" Nan echoed with every evidence of surprise when Donald returned from the bar with more change to feed into the restaurant's pay phone. "No, why?"

Donald distrusted the quality of this denial. As far back as childhood Nan had perfected the art of keeping to the letter of the law but not the spirit. When she said Hattie wasn't there it didn't mean that she hadn't been, or wasn't expected.

"I've been trying to reach her, it occurred to me that I haven't seen her or talked to her in quite a while, and she isn't home."

"Well, she does go places; she isn't a recluse."

It was half challenging, but that had been Nan's mood for the past two months. She had evidently found out what other people had known for some time, that Peter Farris tended to chase and frequently catch other women, and the strain of pretending that these were harmless flirtations had to show up somewhere.

That was why Donald had not asked her if her husband had investigated one of his notebooks. Determined though she might be to keep what she had, that boat would not survive much further rocking.

152

Appearances to the contrary, Nan was thoroughly domesticated. She loved her house and the running of it, the summer sailing, the entertaining that went along with being an account executive's wife. It could be presumed that she also loved Peter, in spite of increasing indiscretion, enough to fight to keep her marriage intact.

Did the indiscretion, Donald wondered for the first time, date back to the revelation of Charlotte Ivy's will?

He was still not going to make any premature mention of Cherry's astonishing hypothesis. He said, "You're right, of course. I suppose I thought that with the snow . . ." and then, in a different and brisker tone, "I have a technical question for Peter, if he's right there."

"No, he's out giving Bravo a walk."

Nan did not add the expected suggestion that Peter call him back. Donald said, "Oh, well, it'll keep," and heard in the near background, just before he hung up, a single deep imperious bark.

So much for walking the German shepherd. How many excuses did Nan have to keep on tap and in careful rotation? The dog, although Peter usually left the bad-weather exercising to her. A working dinner (or on a weekend, lunch) with a client. Or her husband had locked himself up with a problem that had to be settled by morning and would have her head if she interrupted him.

Was it within the bounds of possibility that on this particular night Nan was simply obeying orders: "If anyone calls, I'm out walking Bravo?"

Donald knew exactly where this notion had sprung from. The movie had not been so riveting as to bury Cherry's exact words about her suspicions over Roger.

"I haven't breathed a word to Laurence or Nan." But what about Peter Farris? Although he didn't see a great deal of them all together, it had always seemed to him that there was an exceptional understanding between those two. The natural bond of having married into a family, or because one basic opportunist recognized another? There would certainly have been a shared disappointment over Charlotte's will.

Roger had been stopped in mid-bark late that afternoon. By whom? Only Hattie's car had stood in front of the house, but the driveway continued on behind, past the separate garage. That had been Charlotte Ivy's doing; when she wanted to avoid a bore she simply parked her car out of sight and left the garage doors open on emptiness.

Suppose Hattie had not gone out, as Belinda thought possible, but had been gearing herself to arrive at some kind of agreement with Farris? Oh, come, said Donald to himself, and was rapped sharply on the shoulder with the edge of a coin. He turned to discover a large woman in a woolly brown fez pulled low over her eyebrows, demanding to know if he intended to monopolize the telephone all night.

Upon closer acquaintance it wasn't a fez, it was her hair. Donald, who had spoken to Belinda for two minutes and to Nan for less than that, smiled confidentially at her, said, "One more call should do it," and dialed Laurence's number. Busy.

There was no help for it. Much as he disliked the prospect, he would have to descend on Hattie's house; use her knocker, rattle her doorknob, rap on her windows. The priorities had taken a sudden unpleasant shift, because he had no idea what he had driven away from when he left that abrupt stillness.

How was Hattie, this minute? As unaware as he, until just now, of the possible black pattern locking itself around her?

The house wasn't far, for a crow; to Donald the negotiating of the steep narrow streets before he could leave the center of the town behind him seemed interminable. The lightly whitened and relatively untraveled roads here would either be bare with the first sun or buried in three or four inches of fresh snow; the air had lost its edge and it was hard to tell which way that would go. Surprise snowstorms visited New England with great regularity.

The church corner was less than a quarter-mile away when a car that looked like Belinda's flashed past. Although it couldn't

*154*

be, Donald's foot went instinctively down on the accelerator. The car ahead ignored the stop sign and shot into the path of dangerously close brilliance from the right on River Road.

Donald had to wait for the passage of the oncoming car and another following. By then he had had time to register two facts: that from the rear at least Hattie's house was dark, and with the night black again the car, which had taken a considerable chance, could only be somewhere behind the sweeping spruces that surrounded the church's small cemetery.

Such peculiar behavior so close to his goal warranted a fast look. He entered the lane, caught a broken glimpse of lemon metal between branches ahead and to the left, swung the wheel.

The driver's door in the wash of his lights hung open. Beyond, about to disappear into the night—

He was out of the car with his engine running, calling in a mixture of urgency and disbelief, "Belinda!"

She didn't stop until he had called a second time and, realizing that he was a faceless shape against blasting gold, stepped back a little. Then she came flying to him, her breathing harsh and labored, shivering as his arms went quite naturally around her.

"Norman was after me, and I didn't know what he—" The race of her heart against him was alarming, and Donald stroked her hair. Belinda said disconnectedly and as if it were the ultimate catastrophe, "He did something to the horn."

Even with no idea as to how this set of circumstances had come about, Donald did not need to have that spelled out for him. "Do you have your keys?" he said, deliberately brisk. "Because let's leave your car here and pick it up in the morning."

They were in the ignition; she hadn't paused to remove them. When Donald had installed her on his front seat and returned from the locking up she was calmer; she even gave him a shaky smile in the dashboard glow. "I was going to be so sensible. I wouldn't have fallen into any trap about being needed at my parents' house, but Norman was one step ahead of me."

"Not quite. You're here and he isn't," said Donald, again

refraining from questions. He glanced across at her. "I have to stop at Hattie's, can you hang on for that?"

"Yes. I'm all right now," said Belinda, and the very simplicity of the words was like a treasure delivered into his hands. The absorbence of it made him a pulse beat late in identifying what, poised at the mouth of the church lane, he saw obliquely up the road a hundred yards away.

Just a flicker of flashlight behind the low stone wall across from Hattie's house, extinguished instantly but enough to give him the impression of someone digging.

*Here. Tonight.*

He said to Belinda, fast, "Can you get the flashlight from the glove compartment?" and took the corner so that the car rocked when he slammed on his brakes, received the cylinder in his hand, and got out with the beam flaring, pinning. He said to his brother-in-law, "Don't do it, Peter," and then, "I have a friend, watching, and the police on the way."

"Messy job," said Peter Farris conversationally, as if there had been no false threat. "Poor old Hattie didn't want to watch any part of it, so she's gone to bed."

He moved so that his black shadow covered the fringy dog on the ground. "She called up about a half-hour ago—would I come and bury Roger? He'd gotten loose and been killed in the road, and she'd found a replacement but couldn't live with herself. She's going to let the lawyer know in the morning, but I told her I was sure you and Laurence and Nan wouldn't want to do anything vindictive."

The unavoidable sway of Donald's flashlight as he stepped over the wall had shown him a small grave, dusted with white although the snow had stopped some time ago, and something else. Or had he only imagined that stir, as of a stunned animal trying to lift its head?

He took a chance. With Peter leaning on the dangerous shovel he said, "You're right, we wouldn't." And then, "Did Hattie want you to bury Roger *alive*?"

He had banked on a flick of incredulous glancing down and

*156*

back, and he got it. He made an instant twisting dive, last remembered from his football days, and as the other man went pitching awkwardly over his shoulder he rolled free, picked up the warm little body, got to his feet, negotiated the wall again.

Winded, feeling bruised from head to foot because a typewriter was no training for such encounters, he deposited the dog on the back seat of the car, looked at his hands and gave them a rapid wipe on his handkerchief.

"There's blood somewhere, but he's alive," he said to Belinda's shocked pallor, and, deliberately postponing something, leaned in and kissed her cheek. "Can you drive him to the clinic?"

She slid over behind the wheel without question, sending a terrified glance past him. "But what about—won't he . . . ?"

Farris's head had connected with the wall, and he was up only as far as one knee. "I doubt it," said Donald grimly.

They both heard it at the same time: the sound of running feet in the dark driveway across the road. She didn't pause at the sight of the car, even though the headlights illumined at least part of the scene, but with her scarfed head averted as she ran in the direction of a gold-windowed house where there was a party in progress she was still identifiably Cherry Aintree.

Where to hide the car in case of chance callers on Hattie? In among a lot of others.

"I think we have just seen some state's evidence in the making," said Donald. "Call me here, will you?"

And then, filled with dread, he undertook his own dash for Hattie's black house.

With a note coming due on the loan that Peter Farris had taken out in order to buy oil leases on the strength of his wife's expectations from her elderly aunt, it hadn't been a bad idea. It might well have worked, given Hattie's character, except for last-minute witnesses and the emergency-room treatment, which would have been useless an hour or two later.

The unmistakable digging out of the run. The duplicate dog.

The jotted reminder which could have been an abbreviated suicide note. Perhaps most telling, the mingling of barbiturates and alcohol, which an autopsy would have shown: Hattie, a nurse for most of her life, would know the perils of that combination and appear to have taken the painless way out of a situation she couldn't face. Charlotte Ivy's sleeping pills were still in the medicine cabinet, and of late Nan Farris had been resorting to her own supply.

Nan and Laurence, both innocent, he unaware of a telephone receiver placed slightly askew when Cherry insisted on dropping him off because he wasn't fully recovered from his cold, could have been persuaded to keep silent about the dinner. "Hattie was perfectly compos mentis by the time Cherry undressed her and got her to bed, but, my God, how would it look?"

Who, then, would have thought to take away the black calf mid-heel shoes and the green suit jacket with its silvery buttons on a hanger—woman suicides were generally neat—and find Cherry Aintree's fingerprints on those accommodating surfaces?

Confronted with them, Cherry did some majestic plea bargaining even before she got her lawyer. "Would you," she asked Lieutenant Hallam, "like to know who killed Deborah Kingsley and who gave me a chew stick dipped in a strong insecticide for the dog? Stupid," this with an air of cool divorcement, "but Peter had read about a town in New Mexico where half the pet population had been wiped out that way. Roger could have died while Hattie was asleep or away from the house, and he had been let out of the run; he could have picked up the poison anywhere."

"I'd rather hear about Deborah Kingsley."

"Peter's original plan had been to tie the dog and then run over him," said Cherry with detachment, "but Roger got away from him and then along came that girl, who had a good look at both of them. The will guaranteed an investigation if anything happened to Roger, and I don't see how they could do that without publicity and reward offers, so there was no point in going ahead while the girl was alive. She'd have come forward at once, especially in her job."

"I see that," said Hallam, contriving a certain sympathy so that she would not close up. "But why go after Miss Callahan too?"

"She was getting suspicious, for one thing. Peter figured out what the electrician was for, and she was having new keys made. Pretty soon the dog would have been impossible to get at. And then he thought why not get rid of the whole problem? It isn't usual for a dog to have only one puppy, and chances were that my brother-in-law, Donald Aintree, would have made some note about getting hold of Roger for his aunt."

She was not the first of her kind whom Hallam had met, whipping her skirts fastidiously away from a murderous enterprise in which she had taken full part. Why, he wanted to know, had she cooperated with Peter Farris, a killer; done the telephoning and picked up the dog, which was to be the explanation of Hattie's suicidal remorse?

"Because he had a hold over me. After a party last summer, we—must I spell it out?" Drop of black lashes on fine pale skin; Hallam, watching, thought it curious that no color came along to emphasize distaste and embarrassment. "It was an impulse thing, an isolated occasion, but I was afraid my husband wouldn't believe that."

Hallam didn't believe it either, any of it. This young woman did not strike him as a yielder to impulses, and no sane person would assist with the taking of a life simply to avoid an angry marital scene. Still, he said dryly, "That was a threat that cut two ways, wasn't it?"

The dark gaze came up, confident and a little contemptuous. "Oh, Nan's used to it."

As guilty as Farris, even if it hadn't been her finger on the trigger; perhaps even the architect of the whole scheme. But they did badly want Deborah Kingsley's killer and sometimes it was necessary to look obliquely if not quite the other way.

The evening had brought Hallam one satisfaction that almost wiped out the bitter taste of McFee. In his pursuit of Belinda Grace, and at his speed, Norman Comstock's swerve to avoid a woman backing out of her driveway without benefit of taillights had sent him through a post-and-rail fence. Give him credit, however reluctantly; with another driver there might have been a crash. The enraged fence owner, a fisherman who held a few amateur weight-lifting titles, had detained him while he called the police.

With the growing official concern about arson, Hallam thought that the Bell Falls police would be happy to talk to Comstock, and at some length.

And—nothing to do with the case but increasingly on his mind—could slender Sue be seriously interested in a man with all that stomach? People did change; look at her eating steamed clams.

Call her, say offhandedly that she might be interested in a case he was wrapping up because it centered around a dog?

Think about it.


Roger was longer in the mending than Hattie. The shovel had grazed and bloodied his head and then aimed at his hip, which now carried a few of Dr. Vincent Cooper's skillful steel pins.

He had been made much of at the clinic and subsequently by Hattie's vet, not because he was a joy to behold, like the Maltese terrier, but because of the tale that surrounded him. He had grown bold as a result, leaving his playthings carelessly on the living room rug instead of returning them to his basket, and barking summarily at Hattie when he wanted his dinner. It took a contact with the electric fence to bring him to his senses.

Two marriages would go down the drain, after the punctilious Aintree standing-by had been maintained through the trial. Had either of them, under the circumstances, been worth saving?

"Do you know," said Donald to Belinda in the restaurant where he had taken her to lunch the day before and where something had begun to inform the very air between them, "that apart from finding Hattie as good as dead the worst part of that whole night was when I thought I'd gone mad? There you were, speeding off to the clinic with Roger, and there he seemed to be in Hattie's living room, staring at me.''

"His owners can't be very nice. I can keep him, my building allows pets,'' said Belinda although Boston seemed a moon distance away.

"Another?'' inquired the same waiter, collecting Donald's empty glass. "And for the lady bartender too?''

It was sunny today, and the walls and ceiling of the big dining room quaked with what was no doubt reflected light off the harbor but might equally have been a quivery incandescence generated at their own table. And indeed people were looking at them; knowing, amused, envious, a little nostalgic.

"Please,'' said Belinda.